Henry Iliowizi

Herod

A Tragedy

Henry Iliowizi

Herod
A Tragedy

ISBN/EAN: 9783337187316

Printed in Europe, USA, Canada, Australia, Japan

Cover: Foto ©Andreas Hilbeck / pixelio.de

More available books at **www.hansebooks.com**

HEROD:

A TRAGEDY.

By HENRY ILIOWIZI,

AUTHOR OF SOL.

MINNEAPOLIS, MINN.
1884.

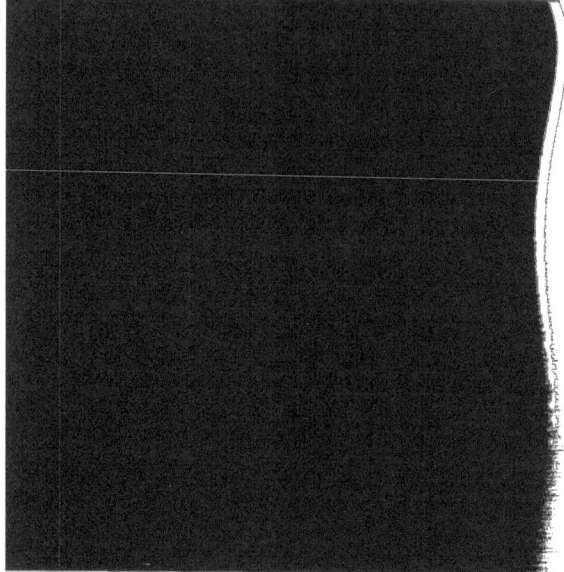

Printed at the Tribune Book
Rooms, Minneapolis, Minn.

SOL:

AN EPIC POEM.

BY

REV. HENRY ILIOWIZI.

St. Paul *Pioneer Press*:—The author treats the subject with much poetical vigor. Beautiful similes abound. Scenes are vividly set forth. Of course in a work of this kind there must be a suggestion of the Divine Comedy, but nevertheless this poem is filled with fresh conceptions eloquently expressed.

Chicago *Journal*:—Mr. Iliowizi's poem, which is the work of years, will be read with interest and pleasure, not only by the people of his own race, but by the Christian also.

The Occident, of Chicago:—The author exhibits a dexterous pen in giving the tragical end of Sol. The lines run smoothly, and much poetic fervor is lent to each canto. Altogether, it presents a very interesting volume, which is neatly printed, and, though not wholly·free from typographical mistakes, will prove a welcome adjunct to modern literature.

The Messenger, of New York:—These thrilling incidents have been skillfully seized upon by the author for his epic. * * * Throughout the book the author displays a force and eloquence which are promising for his future. His style is often pithy and epigramatic, * * * and we feel confident that with study and practice his promising literary gifts will give him a worthy place among writers of the day.

· *The Interior*, of Chicago :—It is certain that Rabbi Iliowizi has given us an epic marked by rare poetical ability,—a grand poem which, while felicitously and powerfully portraying the aspirations, the hopes, the sufferings, and the traditions of his own people in connection with the sad end of Sol, the heroic maiden, forcibly appeals to the warm sympathies and kindly feelings of all Christian people. Gentiles and Jews will read this remarkable epic with almost equal pleasure. All admirers of epic poetry will appreciate and enjoy its majestic movement, its vivid descriptions and its glowing imagery.

To the magnanimous guide and benefactor of my youth,

DR. BÆRWALD,

Director of the Philanthropic Institution in Frankfort-on-the-Main, this production is gratefully inscribed:

My dearest and most revered friend:

The first and most precious benefit I derive from this insignificant composition is the dear opportunity it affords me to inform the world that, but for your generosity and almost fatherly care, I should most probably be one of those unfortunate and unfriended beings whose life is a burden to themselves and mankind. Severed from the semi-barbarous land of my birth and thrown into this world without the least preparation for its unavoidable struggle, you have lifted me from the depth of misery, endured and patiently corrected the aberrations of my youth, brought me near the best sources of learning, and put me beyond the reach of want until a training of ten years spent under your auspices enabled me to face independently the problem of this existence. The longer I am away from you, friend of my soul, and the more the selfish qualities of man's nature become a matter of fact to me, the deeper grows my gratitude to you, and the greater my admiration of that sweet benignity which is the essential feature of your truly humane and great character. Your life is a pure mirror reflecting everything that is divine in man; an ideal to which one may aspire, but which is too lofty for the average mortal. May the Lord bless and preserve you for the good of that vast circle of grateful friends and enthusiastic followers, one of whom I shall in deep devotion, respect and gratitude ever be proud to be.

HENRY ILIOWIZI.

Minneapolis, Minn., April 1, 1884.

ARGUMENT.

Herod, having received the crown of Judea from the hand of Rome, takes Jerusalem by assault, assisted by Sosuis, the Roman general. Although married to a princess of the great Asmonean line. Herod, fearing the popularity of this royal house, resolves to remove all those who have a claim to the throne he usurped; prominent among whom is Hyrcanus, the Queen Mariamne's grandsire, and Aristobulus, her young brother. Having disposed of Antigonus, the conquered and captive King of Israel whom Sosuis leads away in chains. Herod, encouraged by the auspicious prophecy of Manahem, after promoting Aristobulus to the rank of High Priest, causes him to be drowned, and succeeds, under a plausible pretext, to execute Hyrcanus, whom, by captivating promises he lures from Parthia, where the priest lived exiled. These proceedings exasperate Mariamne against Herod, and her hatred becomes uncontrollable on learning that the King, being summoned before Antony to account for Aristobulus' death, secretly ordered Joseph, his sister's husband, to slay the Queen in case Antony would slay him. Finding on his return the Queen in a state of exasperation, and hearing that Joseph has betrayed the secret, Herod, who first doubted Salome's insinuations against her husband's and Mariamne's fidelity, is now convinced that a criminal intimacy existed between his wife, the Queen, and Joseph, whose decapitation he orders at once. Joseph's persistence, however, in denying his guilt to the last, unsettles the conviction of the King, who, dreading the possibility of the Queen becoming an innocent victim of his jealousy, hastens to revoke the order of Mariamne's execution; but the messenger comes too late to arrest the axe of the headsman, and Herod's grief for his adored wife assumes the nature of wild despair. He slays Sabion, who is, by accident, the bearer of the dark tidings; would not hear that the Queen was dead, and st.bs Eurycles, whose words confirm her fall, and who was instrumental in bringing about her sad end. The dying wretch reveals the treacherous scheme laid by Salome for the ruin of the Queen she hated and her husband, and Herod's despair vents itself in his trying to end his life, in which he is prevented by his brother, Pheroras.

DRAMATIS PERSONÆ.

HEROD,	King of Judea.
MARIAMNE,	his wife and Queen.
ALEXANDRA,	her mother.
ARISTOBULUS,	her brother, son of Alexandra, High Priest for a while.
HYRCANUS,	ex-High Priest, father of Alexandra.
PHERORAS,	Herod's brother.
SALOME,	his sister.
JOSEPH,	Salome's husband, treasurer of Herod.
CYPROS,	Herod's mother.
ANTIGONUS,	ex-King of Judea.
DIOPHANTUS,	Herod's secretary.
SARAMELLAS,	his ambassador.
CORINTHUS,	his captain of the guards.
PHABATUS,	his steward.
EURYCLES,	a creature.
PHRAATES,	King of Parthia.
SOSIUS,	a Roman general.
SABION,	confidant of Alexandra.
ÆSOP,	her servant.
MATTHIAS,	the High Priest.
JUDAS SERIPHEUS,	a teacher of the law.
MANAHEM,	a leader of the Essenes.

A physician, captains, headsmen, messengers, citizens, scholars, a deputation of elders, guards, children, and other persons.

The scene is mainly in Jerusalem, with the exception of three scenes, one laid in Jericho, the other in Parthia, the third in Athens.

HEROD.

ACT I.

SCENE I.

Jerusalem. A room in the palace.

Enter Herod, Pheroras, Diophantus, Corinthus, *and a train of armed officers, as coming from the fight.*

Herod. Ungirt my sword, Corinthus; bid the guards
Deny access to the oppressed crowds;
But friends well tried admittance have to us,
Though not with our consent the Romans slay.

> [*Corinthus ungirts Herod and leaves with the officers.*

Pher. This hour to rest be given, king; the task
Most arduous in its kind is done, and now
Our allies teach thy foes obey; the tongues
That loud against thy rule declaimed are mute.

Her. This bloody harvest lames our kingdom's weal,
Pheroras. Have we the power not ourselves
Of minor foes our throne to rid, now that
The head of them is in the Roman's grip?
Proceed at once the legions' harshness check!
Haste, prince, haste all, and curb the slayers' rage,
Even before I Sosius meet.—Outline
A list of them to be removed, and let
The treacherous heads me count before they fall—

> (*Aside to Pheroras.*)

Go, send me Sosius here, who deals as if
He lightly rated our supreme command.
We shall bespeak him plain whom Antony
To conquer not to slay this people sent.

> [*Exeunt Pheroras and Diophantus.*

Thus are my visions verified at last,
And I am lifted on great Solomon's throne,
With Rome as pillar to uphold my state!
When gods combine the mortal to extol,
To raise the lowly to some lofty height,
They first with soaring instincts him endow,
The heart to wish, the boldness to aspire,
The nerve to strive, the triumph to achieve,
And rule he will whom heavenly powers back!

Thus crowned with victory the diadem
I hold, and no proud Asmonean shall wrest
It from my grasp! The high priest not, the sword
Now sways the world, Hyrcanus, and thy days
Of sanctimonious fame are past. A man
Of humble parentage thy priestly robe
Shall wear with all the mystic signs which thrill
The slavish crowds. Thy trimmed ears, old man,
Jehovah will by miracles not round,
And he thy place shall fill whom Herod's whim
With sanctity invests.—Yet nearer me
That ex-priest I prefer, where less his right
To his inheritance I apprehend
Than while he dwelleth at the Parthian court.
A call of love will hither lure him soon
Where at my ease I may dispose of him.--
The royal offsprings yet by scores must go
Ere I Judea can my kingdom call,
And joyous hearts will break with grief and woe
By anguish rent for those who still must fall.
What comes—Corinthus?   [*Enter Corinthus.*
    Cor.   Manahem begs to see
The King, and so he urges that with him
I beg.
    Her. Let him appear who upright is in heart
And in the stars the future's course can read.— [*Enter Manahem.*
The possible be thine. Manahem, speak!
    Mana. King, fear the Ruler of thy destiny;
With dead the town is cloyed, the lanes with gore,
The heathens slay the mother and the babe,
Defile the Sanctuary's sacred seats,
The virgin outrage, plunder every house,
And thou art silent, hast no word for them
Whose guiltless blood may imprecations call
Upon those hordes who thus thy cause befoul!
    Her. Shame on those warriors who such havoc make!
Accuse me not, oh righteous man, my heart
Not less doth for Judea bleed than thine.
It is Jerusalem my capital
They devastate, and those they slay are all
My subjects dear. Twelve messengers are out
To seek the chief and Sosius, ere a while,
I here expect. Yet curse not such as deal
With you as foes; that prince condemn who by
His treason brought on you this woe. Not me,
Manahem, not Herod, but Antigonus
Arraign, who is now punished for his base
Designs.
    Mana. Not all the wrong is his, my lord,
Though many are the errors of that prince.
He for the kingdom of his fathers strove
And no allegiance to the Roman owed;
But Heaven decreed it so, and so it be.
    Her. His brother's birthright boldly he usurped,
And Israel's high priest he outraging maimed.
Five hundred maidens he to Parthia gave
Had I not thwarted his atrocious plans.

The martyr's death through him my Phassel died,
Whose blood to Heaven loud for vengeance cries!
Mana. His fate is sealed ; I know Antigonus
By pagan hand must fall, and thus the last
Of great Asmoneus' brilliant house will end,
A captive with no child, no friend, no priest
To weep a tear or for his body care.—
Be moved, O king, by that mysterious Might
Who plays with thrones as boys with insects play;
Be moved, and grant the satisfaction me
Of being near him when abroad he dies;
For nothing done is in this nether world
Of which a record is not kept above.
Her. And wouldst thou follow him to Rome and see
Him there Antonius' triumph grace? Bethink
Thyself, it is a distant way.
Mana.   Thy care
Will not permit him Italy to view;
And were it otherwise I should to Rome
Accompany the prince.
Her.   Manahem, thou art
A man inspired by the Lord; in me
Thy prophecies are verified; I am
Judea's king as thou didst once foretell.
Thou shalt not vainly wish, if I can help;
Antigonus shall die by thee consoled.—   [*Exit Manahem.*
Thus smile the stars and victory and Rome
On me, and thou, Antigonus, art doomed
To be the worm's repast, to disappear
When Herod says Depart! Yea, Rome, thou shalt
Not see, nor have a chance to plead thy cause
Much stronger than the mine if justice ruled.—
Or should I mine plebeian birth compared
See with his line, his right to reign see on
The scale with mine? Antipater, my sire,
Would in his grave blush at this dotish boy
If I on claims would dare my throne to found.
The world with fallen royalty may sigh,
But hath no sympathy with upstart knaves
Who rise by force and must by force subsist.
Thus force shall bring thee to the dust, my prince!
Antonius must in this my purpose serve;
The others here I shall in time remove,   [*Enter Sosius.*
And clear this nest of its patrician brood.—
There Sosius comes, who shall my ends promote —
What means that slaughter of the infants, man ?
Art thou here sent with girls and babes to war,
So slay my people, plunder house and fane
And leave me monarch of a desert land ?
The Roman empire can that blood not pay
Thy wild centurians shed in vain this day.
Sos. The worst is done the warrior to appease,
Who of his triumphs justly claims a share.
They are restrained who thus the king displeased.
Her. Not one of them shall leave my kingdom poor,
But none should say that Herod's friends are such
As reverence lack for innocence and gods.

To Rome my crown, to her I friendship owe
And would not thus her glory tarnish'd see
By acts barbarians would too cruel deem.
   Sos Such licence, king, the Roman oversees.
The soldier's life is fraught with risk and pain;
Each day. each hour new dangers he must face,
Must ghastly death in thousand shapes confront,
Without the prospect of a peaceful grave,
And this for them who crowns and sceptres crave;
What price can pay such self-denying zeal?
   Her. No price buys valor which a world subdues.
   Sos Which asks not who but where the foe doth lie,
And shrinks not back when orders bid to die.
   Her. The Roman warrior will the wonder be
Of generations yet to come, and learn
What giant races ruled in olden times.
If I on prowess could rely as this
How easy would my head and slumbers be.
   Sos. Thy friends are wakeful while thou art asleep;
What Rome hath given she but can retract;
Her friends against a world she can protect
   Her. My crown she can, my head she cannot save,
My breast once pierced she could not knit again,
And this—oh let me plainly speak—this haunts
Me day and night as long as he ——
   Sos.   As he?
Who is the he alarming Herod's rest?
   Her. As long as I Antigonus must fear.—
   Sos. Can Herod fear a craven, captive prince!
   Her. Stood he within my dagger's reach I feared
Him not
   Sos.   What is it Herod fears?
   Her.   There lives
No being in this world I truly fear
Who fear no death. But lifted on a throne
There is the million-headed beast untamed,
A monster knowing no surcease in rage,
Beseiging me with poison in its look.
That beast whom Brutus dreaded makes me think,
Good Sosius; mark—the rabble is for him.
   Sos. The rabble! Cannot Judea's dregs be quelled,
He being far?
   Her.   Will never rest until they know
Him in the dark beyond. They will not rest
But plague me with unending schemes and plots
And this would make a Cæsar shrug with doubt.
   Sos. Antonius is thy friend, and what in this
I in thy favor may secure depend
On me.
   Her. Nay, all thy favors would be crowned
By this, without which all, I grieve to say,
Are half. His death alone our triumph makes
Complete.
   Sos.   Count on a soldier's word.
   Her.   [*grasping Sosius' hand.*] Here with
This hand accept my grateful heart! Twelve loads
Of gold I to thy care entrust, let four

Be thine, the rest thy master's due; aud ere
Thy valiant legions Jerusalem forsake
A fifty talents shall their zeal reward.
  Sos. I thank thee, monarch, for the royal gifts,
And shall remember what I Herod owe.   *[Will go.*
  Her. One word.—A pious man, a favorite
Of mine, Manahem, who my rule foretold
Some twenty years ago, predicting came
To me, imploring that he may be there
Where fate decreed Antigonus should fall.
Allow that man the captive to approach,
His ardor being to console the prince.
  Sos. The guard shall be instructed on this point.   *[Exit.*
  Her. Now thee I seek, sweet goddess of my soul,
Mariamne, princess of my self and all.
In my new crown thou art the precious gem;
Thy love is more than this world's diadem!

SCENE II.

A room.

Enter DIOPHANTUS *with papers, and* SARAMELLAS.

  Diophantus. Thou hast no time to waste, Saramellas;
The king dislikes in this affair delay;
The message should be there and auswer here
Before the moon is full. Art thou prepared
To start for Parthia's court?
  Saramellas.   Prepared! Who could
In minutes for an embassy prepare?
I am surprised that I am chosen for
The mission named. I would another had
The trust reluctant to my peaceful mood.
  Dio The king is restless till he Parthia knows
Appeased, knows old Hyrcanus out of Phraates
Reach. Get here the priest, the monarch wills
No more. Thy prudence use as ladder to
Thy fortune's top.
  Sara.   I go unwilling to
The Parthian court; I loathe Pacorus more
Than he doth Rome: yet meet I shall that chief
And him who rules, and face all perils which
The task beset, although the prize is but
An ear-trimm'd priest.
  Dio.   Whom thou must promise half
Of Herod's throne who sends for him to pay
A filial due.
  Sara.   By hugging him until
He dreams in bliss.——I have a pity for
That hoary head whose friends so coarsely do
His love requite.
  Dio.   Thou canst not Herod serve
And Heaven, friend. Like Janus double-faced
Thou at this court alone canst thrive; but with
A conscience whispering in thee thou art
Not born a courtier's role to play. Go, climb
Thy hill. This turn of times leaves room for lords

To rise or those who wisely serve their ends.
Let grandam scruples not thy mind desturb
Nor virtuous sickuess pale thy prospects bright.
Thy rule be caution, thy reward success.
Farewell! The hour is pressing and the task
Undone. Farewell, and here these letters take.   [*Exit.*

 Sara. Farewell, shrewd man, Saramellas no guilt
Will on his conscience load. A courtier may
Yet thrive and be a mtu. I let these letters
But not my speech suspectless age decoy.
I see the plot against the luckless prince
Whom I should lure into a guileful snare.
I nor my skill shall nor my suasion strain
If thou, Hyrcanus, wilt the bait disdain;
But age is dotish when the passions sway,
And thou, I fear, wilt Herod's call obey.   [*Exit.*

SCENE III.

A street in Jerusalem.

Enter Citizens from different sides.

 1st Citizen. [*to one passing by*] Stop neighbor, halloo, stop!
  what the deuce! Has he
The feathered sickness in his limbs?—Stop, Ezra!
Why, man, one would suppose a Roman close
Behind thee.—Well, how about the newest news?
They are away, eh?
 2d Cit.   The Romans?
 1st Cit.   Yes, the Romans.
The fever shake the Romans! Are they all
Away, the wolfish heathens, all away?
 2d Cit. Ay, Gamliel, or such an airing would prove hot
for us. They are all gone, the dogs; have seen
Myself them marching out of town on foot,
On horse, by dreaded Sosius led who rode
Triumphant, while the drums and flutes discoursed.
 1st Cit. The pest on Sosius whose insatiate greed
Was glutted by the tyrant at our cost.
Four camels bore Judea's gold for him,
And eight for Antony our treasures took,
While every soldier got a heavy boon.
They chased our maidens not and wives in vain,
Nor slew our babes without the due reward
By him bestowed who on our marrow lives!
And we like slaves endure outrageous wrong
And wonder at the hateful yoke we bear.
 3d Cit. Exasperated once the tribes will rise
And shake the bloody tyrant off their neck.
We are no slaves and shall not bear it loug.
 Other Cits. We are no slaves and shall not bear it long.
 1st Cit. Did ye Antigouus in chains not see
Degraded by a bondslave's coarse attire?
 One of the crowd. I did, I did!
 Others   We did not see him, no!
 2d Cit. I did, I did as here I see my hand.
He had his palms upon his royal face

And linked to a wagon he paced along,
Behind a guard, before him Sosius on
A prancing steed. All who beheld him pass
Bemourned him as lost. Manahem was
With him.
 All. Manahem!
 1st Cit.   Ah, Manahem, best
Of souls! In thee Jerusalem bewails
An upright heart!—Was he with him? Why, such
A man as would for pity's sake not kill
A fly disporting on his nose, and nurse
To patients was whose foul pestiferous couch
Their nearest kindred frightened from their side!
Why him, of the Essenes the righteous head,
Select from thousands for a boudman's lot,
Let others answer give.
 2d Cit.   No bondman he,
Digest it better, man; but here the hinge.
You see how flesh unlike is flesh. Tell me
To face a Roman or confront a wolf,
I face the beast; but then a pious man
Is not of common flesh, and so Manahem.—
The prince must not unwept be slain, so thought
Manahem, and besought the king to speak
A kindly word for him, which, being done,
He got the privilege to go and weep.
 3d Cit. He was himself predicting Herod's rule.
 2d Cit. When clouds are frowning swallows prophesy
And when it showers fools can say: It rains.—
Had not Hyrcanus such a vampire nursed
There would be none to suck his royal blood.
What can he be, his nursling being king?
 1st Cit. Ask better, what, the priesthood being lost?
His maim unfits him for the sacred trust,
And gossip says his substitute is named.
 3d Cit Pray who is he destined to rule the Shrine?
 2d Cit. I know the man not, though his name I heard.
 3d Cit. Is he not one of Asmoneus' line
Whose progeny by right the altar tread?
 2d Cit. May be, may be, some lines do far extend,
Although Ananelus no kinship claims
With the descendants of the Maccabees.   [*Sabion enters.*
 1st Cit. Ananelus? Why, Sabion there will tell—
Is not Ananelus a Greek by name?
 Sabion. Ananelus? I never heard this name.
 Other Cit. We never heard the name, he is a Greek.
 1st Cit. Well, what of that? The king is Greek in all
And wants all heathen customs planted here,
And with a high priest of the Grecian race
The way for Jupiter and Bacchus paved
Is to our Sanctuary's holiest seat.
Thus far we by degrees arrive. He will
Not stop where he is now. Why, dotards as
We are, should he bethink himself when him
The fashion goads?
 Sab. [*to the 1st Cit.*] What made thee guess the king
Would tear the priesthood from the Asmoneans?

1st Cit. I am no guesser, but I know the fact;
Ananelus the king installed as priest.
From Babylon he came by Herod called
Who did the holy office him entrust
And all the titles of the sacred rank.
It was a secret which is known to-day
And old Hyrcanus may his looks unhair.
Sab. Brothers, there is nor gratitude nor love
Nor friendship in this world; and if of these
There be a mite in beastly substance, man
Of all the beasts in them the poorest seems.
The cat, the dog is grateful; tigers lick
The hand of him who satiates their maw,
But man can flay the generous hand that gives
Destroy the giver and the gift indu'ge.
Each day, it seems, the times are growing worse
And parents should their infants' love suspect.   [*Exit.*
1st Cit. There is a weight and sense in this discourse.
He speaks the truth if one considers well.
It seems that all is tumbling out of joint.
A babe in Hebron came with teeth to light
And scared his mother with unearthly talk.
Some persons passing by the Dead Sea saw
A wondrous castle floating on its waves,
And hellish noise and laughter issued from
Within, and: Herod, Herod! horribly
They heard with hisses and with yelling mixed.
The hens are crowing and the ravens sing,
An Idumean is Judea's king.
All. [*singing*] The hens are crowing and the ravens sing,
An Idumean is Judea's king.   [*Enter a crowd in haste.*
A voice. Protect us, Heaven! Flee for life! Flee, flee!
They slay like sheep the citizens they catch!
                                        [*Exeunt all.*

   Enter PHERORAS *with officers and soldiers.*
Pher. That rabble overtake and cut them off.
The spies report them adverse to the king.
                              [*An officer and soldiers go.*
I seek the others massing somewhere else.
Have all the portals guarded till the game
Is down. They court the chase and shall enjoy .
The sport. We sweep that crowded quarter where
Conspiracy, they say, is ever ripe. [*Pheroras and soldiers leave.*

     SCENE IV.

   A room in the palace.

  ALEXANDRA, ARISTOBULUS, *and* MARIAMNE.

Arist. Had I Saramellas accompanied
With me the grandsire would straightway return;
But mother thinks I am securest home,
As if all roads infested were with wolves
And I no pluck had to defend myself.
Was David older when he Goliath fought?
An idle life like mine the body and
The mind unnerves. I am too fat to move,

And should this hour I die of all the world
Jerusalem and Jericho I viewed
And these but half. How old must be a man
To have his will if I be yet too young?
 Alex. As old as one who wills but what is wise,
And wise is in good season, child. Oh, my son,
Would I could give you what but age can give!
How dear must man for sound experience pay,
And, having it, the chance to use it goes;
Nor can this treasure be an heir's bequest,
Who, in his turn, oft gathers it in vain.—
The world and man are not what they to youth
Appear, dear son. A parent's frown, as cloud
Impregnate with the blessed rain, portends
No evil, though the sight be dark, while smile
On stranger's visage oft that glaring blaze
Resembles which the earthquake's outburst doth
Precede. Intrusive friendship, son, distrust.
Thy secrets bury in thy inmost heart.
And shun those natures who promotion crave
Unscrupulous in choice of means and ways.
Suspect the love of them who rule by force;
They are not human who the weak oppress.
A dragon rather than a talebearer hug;
The glossy tongue of menial courtlings hate.
Trust Heaven, son, and then thy mother's care.
 Mari. So solemn and sententious is thy speech,
Dear mother, as if treason lurking were
Around, and we the vanquished were to-day
And not the victors by Almighty's grace.
Is not Judea Herod's conquered land,
Who loves thy daughter more than life and throne?
Suggest the dignity thy son may wear
And I shall answer for the best result.
This morn he of our grandsire in Parthia spoke
With filial gratitude, affection true.
He hath a heart, I find; since, had he none,
How could soft love invade an iron breast?
 Arist- [*to Mariamne*] And when may we the grandsire's return
Expect? I am impatient to behold
His face who in his arms did fondle me
As babe. He is the best of men on earth!
 Mari. He may return before the moon is round.
A gorgeous escort left this noon for him
With all the comforts of a royal train.
The king is longing to embrace his friend
With whom he means the kingdom to divide.
 Arist. Yet must he not the sacred altar tread,
Must not the people bless with outstretched hand
Which will our joy curtail, mar his delight.
 Alex. Our full affection will his age suffice,
Who will instruct thee how to fill his place.
Thine is the priesthood, son; thy grandsire will
His holy vesture thee not grudge who art
My child and of his flesh and blood. It is
His wish to see the sacred emblems on
Thy breast.

Arist.   Would he could wear them; I could wait;
Am yet too young to awe a pious flock.
    Mari. So spoke the king when I besought him straight
With priestly state Aristobulus to
Invest.
    Alex. Is not my son entitled to
The high priest's robe and the anointment of
Our great ancestral line? A grandchild of
Hyrcanus none can his inheritance
Dispute. He is the priest by Heaven and earth
Approved!
    Mari. I see not who hath stronger claim
Than he, and what the king disturbs is but
His youth, whom he, besides, doth love with all
A brother's heart. I shall not rest before
His scruples yield and my entreaties long
He can't resist. He wields Judea and
I wield his heart, and test I shall how deep
His love to me.
    Alex.   Daughter, if thou must ask,
Entreat, beseech for what by right is ours
Then all thy arts employ before the worst
Is done; for once proclaimed, anointed, none
A high priest can of sanctity divest,
Except a fatal accident. My son
The sacred plates must wear as rightful heir
To what his grandsire should by right bestow.
    Mari. It is the hour for me to see the king,   [*Sabion enters.*
And I this favor ask to test his love
Which hitherto no tongue had to refuse.
Aristobulus shall the mitre wear
And be Judea's ever-blessing priest.
    Sab. And thou Judea's ever-blessed queen.—
Depart not, madam, ere old Sabion spoke.
A startling rumor bid me hither haste
To learn the tidings people whisper round.
The sacred office—so am I apprised—
The king bestowed on one from Babylon.
    Alex. Bestowed? Didst thou not say bestowed?
    Mari.   Bestowed!
He saying this knows more than what is true,
More than of the king's plans the queen doth know. [*Æsop enters.*
    Alex. Speak, Æsop, for thou hast to speak, I see.
    Æsop. My princess, is Ananelus, the priest,
Of Asmonean descent?
    Alex.   Ananelus!
Is that his name who tramples on my son?   [*to Sabion.*
    Sob. He is from Babylon, Ananelus,
On whom the king the priesthood did bestow.
                                        [*Marianne leaves.*
    Alex. Ananelus, thou art my evil star!
My son's disgrace, my father's grief and mine,
And woes impending which will sure evolve
Will bear thy name, Ananelus, to me
Unblest, though bless thou mayst the senseless throngs!
Ungrateful king! Do we so little count
In thy designs that thou darest thus our claim

And station slur? Even a fly can sting,
Why not a woman's vengeance ruin bring?
Invulnerable thou art not, my lord,
And there are powers mightier than thy sword.—
Go, friends, I ought to be alone, I feel;
Dear Sabion, go! I shall requite thy zeal.
　　　　　　　　　[*Sabion, Æsop and Aristobulus go.*
Fair Cleopatra, Antony thy slave
Can all a globe not thy entreaties brave;
Through thee I ask the priesthood not alone,
But for my boy I claim Judea's throne.
Straightway I write my grievance to my friend,
By Egypt's help my son shall rule this land.　　　　　[*Exit.*

SCENE V.

A house in Babylon.

Enter HYRCANUS *and* SARAMELLAS.

Hyrcanus. Have read the letters and my heart is touched
So tender is the breath of love in them.
He calls me father, benefactor, guide,
Would not without my princely aid be king;
Without my wisdom, venerable age.
A son could not be more affectionate
Than he, a stranger to my house and heart,
Save that my grandchild's consort he is now.
I am not sorry I did raise him well
Who full deserves the kingly rank he holds.
He hath a grateful soul, I see he hath.—
And how did Parthia's king the message take?
　　Sara. Thou hast in Phraates quite a friend, my lord.
He is unwilling to behold thee part,
Would not on Herod's promise much rely,
Hopes that thy welfare was secure at home,
And would no hindrance raise if thou wilt go.
He will be here to give thee royal choice.
　　Hyr. If I would go! Would I could borrow of
The eagle speed to wing along and see
My darlings home! Oh, friend, a time of gloom
I spent in this exile, and ofttimes wished
I were among the dead. If life hath worth
It lies in those we love, and none of these
Were here to cheer my age. Though Phraates did
Me hospitably treat my soul was sad,
And oft the tears did flow when I at night
For peace the skies besought, and thought of them
Who in Jerusalem ever sighed for me.
I pardoned him who thus my figure maimed.
But Heaven avenged my undeserved disgrace,
And for his crime Antigonus atones.—　　　　[*Enter deputation.*
Our brethren dwelling here did spare no pains
To link my soul to them by marks of love.
They are deploring my departure hence,
And I regret them but I cannot stay.—
Step nearer, friends, I guess your mission's purport.

1st Elder. [*kissing Hyrcanus' robe*] Oh bide with us whom we
    so deeply love!
Our high priest and our guide art thou, and all
Who on Euphrates' banks Jehovah praise
Beseech thee through my lip to stay with us.
    2d Eld. Forsake us not who far from Zion dwell,
But be our light on Babylonian soil.
    3d Eld. Depart not, sir, remain with us as head.
They have the Temple and thy priestly house,
And many sages there the law expound;
We have but thee our age and youth to teach,
And with thy going all our light withdraws!
    Hyr. You move my soul, I go reluctant hence,
Yet go I must now that my dearest call.
The One Supreme will be your priest and guide,
And bless you for the kindness shown to me.
Here stands the messenger Judea's king
Did send to lead me where my heart was chained,
While thus exiled I yearned for my home.
No, urge me not, dear friends, an impulse to
Subdue which in man's nature is, forsooth,
The best. Your hearths and children bind ye here
And I from mine, alas! am separate
Too long. And should the best of men whose love
Invokes, should I my rights inherited
Disdain, not great Judea with her king,
With Herod not in common rule divide?
    1st Eld. Not all is selfishness which prompts us, sir,
Thus to dissuade thee from departing hence.
Couldst thou as priest the holy office hold,
As monarch mount thy sire's glorious throne
But half our grief would be to miss thee here,
Knowing that Israel by thee is blessed.
But since thy maim precludes thee from the Ark,
Remember, sir, that Herod is a man
On whom perchance thou dost rely too much.
    2d Eld. Thy honors here are not inferior, sir,
To what at best thou mayst expect at home.
Come they to us who would with thee abide,
A royal treatment we to all secure
Who kinship claim with thy illustrious house.
    3d Eld. On height of fortune potentates forget
The favors they, when humble, did receive,
And hate as debtors gratitude to feign
Unbearable to inflated state and pride.
Thy arm is weak, thou must on him depend
Who is usurper of thy native rights,
And whom thy honored presence galling may
Excite. He will thy hoary head not spare
Who in revenge the Holy Synod slew.
    Hyr. Unfounded fear! He ever was my friend
And went to Rome to advocate my cause,
But was promoted 'gainst his will and hope.
His inexperience forces him to seek
What I of statecraft gathered in my time.

Either with him or I myself may rule.—
Is not the errand worded as I say? |*to Saramellas.*
  Sara. The letters state it clear.—There comes the king.

PHRAATES *and train enter on one side, the deputation leave on
                   the other.*

  Hyr. This honor, king, my gratitude makes poor.
I came a captive to thy warlike land
Prepared to die a dark, inglorious death,
And to thy hospitable grace I owe
That I once more my dearest may behold,
And then forever close mine eyes in peace.
  Phra. Not ere the choicest blessings of the skies
Alight on thy anointed head.—Thou art
The priest of the Most High, and royalty
Did awe us in thy look when thee we met
With undisguised intent; wherefore we wished
To treat thee as befits a prince.   Now are
We come to let thee have thy choice.   Our court
And treasures open stand for thee if thou
With us wilt bide whom we revere as friend;
If not, as friend return to them who own
Thy heart.
  Hyr.   This generous way encumbers me,
Oh, king, with weight of royalty I scarce
Can bear.   I go a debtor to thyself and land,
And shall thy kindness on my heart engrave.
As oft as for mankind I Heaven beseech
The king of Parthia shall remembered be,
Whose noble virtues emulation rouse.
Though high priest I of thee I learned much.
Thy grace in giving multiplied the gift
And made the moments of thy presence sweet.
Yea, Heaven doth through monarchs chastise man
Or bless him in the ruler he obeys.
Each land, each people mirror but their kings
Who may their gods or may their demons be.—
May ever Parthia and Judea thrive
As friendly allies in the works of peace,
Be ruled by kings of mutual rivalry
In deeds of love each other to eclipse.
  Phra. The more thy worth we know the less do we
Thy hasty parting like.   It is thy wish
To go we grant, else Herod's urging would
Us find unmoved.   And wouldst thou not with us
Abide who thus unwilling part with thee?   •
  Hyr. As when a daughter from her mother parts
To find a home beneath a lover's roof,
She feels her parent's dotage, weeps with her,
Yet clings with fondness to her husband's breast,
So I, O king, would fain divide myself
Could I my trunk as I my soul divide
Betwixt thyself and them I mostly love.
But when my inmost fervors I consult,
I needs must say that they all hither tend
Where first the beam of heaven struck my sight,
Where all is treasured what my heart enshrines.

I long to die where once my cradle stood,
By them environed who are part of me.
   Phra. [*grasping Hyrcanus' hand*] Then' part'with honor and
     my friendship take,
And may the future not thy hopes deceive.   [*To*[*Saramellas.*
'Tell brother Herod we his craving share
To see henceforth our kingdoms leagued in peace.
                          [*Exeunt Phraates*:*and train.*
   Hyr. Thus are we going, though I truly part
Against a whisper warning in my heart.   [*Exeunt both.*

SCENE VI.

A hall in the palace.

HEROD *and* MARIAMNE.

   Mari. All chat; the pith and gist of love is love
By deeds sustained. Not thus doth Antony
Fair Cleopatra love as if the phrase
Was equal to the gift bestowed. He rules
Her self, she rules the half of earth through him.
The Roman hero all can give he hath, ·
For great in manhood he is great in heart.
Can Herod boast of such unselfishness?
   Her. Mariamne, princess of Judea's lord,
The air I breathe, my rank, my sword, myself
Are thine! And should in kingdoms I mine love
Express when I know well that continents
Are poor to serve as figures when my heart
Computes! Base Cleopatra trades in love
As coin, and for her charms she deems the world
A price; but had great Antony thy price
To pay, the orbs of heaven hardly would
Suffice to buy the bliss a smile of thine
Imparts, so dear and precious seems to me
Thy worth. I am a beggar, queen, if thou
Makest love a debt, and thinkst my soul no price
For thy sweet self.
   Mari.   I set no price for what
I freely gave when grandsire Herod named
To be in life and death, in times or bright
Or dark, my lord. My widowed mother founds
Her hopes on thee; on thee Hyrcanus all
His castles builds. Resemble not that isle
On dolphin's back which, fast submerging, wrecks
A hopeful crowd too confident of what
They thought a rock. I am a stranger to
Thy deep-laid schemes, and with the vulgar do
I startled gaze when Herod's plans behold
The light of day. Doth woman live to warm
Her husband's bed, be like a plaything to
A moody babe who fondles it or throws
It to the winds? Is such the contract of
Devoted love?
   Her. Thou canst not blame me, love,
For such neglect who have no secret hid
Which fits a lady's ear. Forgetfulness

Sometimes doth on attention draw; yet think
I not my memory so dull as not
To wing apace with fondest love. Disprove
It, pigeon, and I will amend.
   Mari.   Amend!
Dost thou not promise more than thou canst do?
  Her. Not less, my love, than I can do I grant.
  Mari. Then grant the priesthood from my brother torn
Against thy promise and this nation's will,
Against thy love the heavens could not buy.
Oh great in words how dwarfish are thy deeds
Who stars canst squander, not thy love of self!
  Her. Can such a thing a cherub move to wrath?
  Mari. It is an outrage which the skies resent!
And speak of love not when with sneering leer
Thou dost thine irony on weakness whet.
  Her. Mariamne, Mars in terrors clad I dare
Confront, but am a kid when Amor clouds
His brow, whose darts forever wounding pierce
My heart and make a love-sick, whining boy
Of me. Come smile again, my queen, for this
Thy frown my welkin's glare bedims, and all
Is chaos when my love is gloom. Come, love,
I will Aristobulus higher than
The altar lift, for which he is too young.
The people would revolt if I a boy
Invested with that awful sanctity
Which hitherto but hoary heads haloed
  Mari. My brother is by birth the rightful priest,
My lord, and all Judea waits to see
Him in the sacred robe our fathers wore.
None thinking him by youth disqualified.
Nay, bitter enmity engender will
This huge disgrace cast on the Asmoneans.
And disaffected will thy people stand
As long as force usurps the place of right.
Thou canst thy will impose, my lord, but love
And honor naught but loyal actions win.—
This will be news for him who Parthia left
By thee invited to be king at home.—
Great Heaven, I see afar a night ascend;
A dreary future rising dark I see,
Which, spreading, veils in gloom this holy land,
This flagrant act it opes the tragedy.   [*Exit Mariamne.*
  Her. (*following her with his eyes*) It opes the tragedy, Mari-
    amne, yes.
Dark incidents are being hatched to fill
The drama I perforce must play. How wilt
Thou startle when my plans are well matured!
Thou seest the egg-shell, not the snake within,
Which, bursting forth, will horrify thy sense
So dreadful is that monster's hellish thirst,
Who conjured comes to swill thy kindred's blood.
Thy love to lose this thought I cannot bear,
But how my lofty station hold amid
A crowd of scions nobler than myself?
The cream are they and I the sediment;

How could I loyally defeat my foes
Who right and habit have all on their side?
Like hydra heads the royal dandies spring
And no Alcides lives to check the crop.—
The morals of the barking world I scorn;
It bows in awe before the unsheathed sword;
The steel can bridle disaffected mobs;
But what the Roman lion makes a lamb,
A creature of his mistress' brow, that spell
Is whelming when a seraph lours, which thou
Art, sylph, to that Egyptian harlot.—Yield
Or not yield. Herod, the battle is not won
As long as thou must yield. A woman's toy,
Although I her adore, I shall not be!—
And if I yield, Mariamne, tremble when
Dread majesty reluctant bows! My love to thee
Can much effect, but—aye, when pliant Jove
To Semele did yield she found her ruin
In his consuming love.—A messenger!
What, news from Antony?   [*Messenger enters.*
    Mess.   From Athens do
I come, and in this paper Antony
Doth speak, my lord.   [*Hands a paper and leaves.*
    Her. [*reads*] " To please Judea's king we will
Antigonus remove, and would be pleased
To have the princely youth, Aristobulus,
Near us before we him promote."—It smells
Not well; there is a piece of Dellius' and
Of Cleopatra's cunning in this broth.
That helps thee to the mitre, boy —Promote
The youth! I know the lusty Roman who,
Though great in field, is sottish when a whore
Doth smile on him, and mocketh nature's law
When virile beauty doth provoke his lust.—
Why not?—A boy and strumpet both beloved
May soon undo what I in years have done.—
Hold, Antony, thou shalt not thwart my schemes;
Ananelus, retire for a while
And let us yielding all those fools beguile.   [*Exit*

SCENE VII.

A prison in Athens.

Enter ANTIGONUS, MANAHEM *and a Headsman.*

Ant. Oh Manahem, Manahem, so must I end
The last of Asmoneus' glorious line
With shame opprobrious on my memory heaped!—
Oh dreadful is thy judgment, Lord, who dost
Oft mortals lift to deepen but their fall!—
Unchain my freedom, headsman, let unbound
Me breathe a while. No tiger could these walls
Surmount. Why should this jail be witness of
My shame? Is this a man of flesh and blood?   [*To Manahem.*
    Heads. Behold the sun before thy chains are off,
Since being off thy head must down at once;
So bid my orders; I have to obey.
    Mana. But for a while suspend the fateful blow

And let the king not unprepared depart.—   [*To Headsman.*
Thy precious seconds waste not, noble prince,
And reconcile thyself with Heaven and earth.
                  [*The chains are taken off.*
   Ant. Oh, call me coward, yet I hate to die ,
The basest stigma withering my name.
He called me Antigone whom I could slay,
Instead of which I knelt to my disgrace.
I was a villain and a base poltroon
Else would I pierce that chest to pity strange.
It would be fame to fall on Sosius' trunk.
Oh wretched instinct which still clings to life
When life is agony and death relief.—
The beast in us, Manahem, not the god
Predominates when we despised must fall.
   Mana. If thus in wreckage thou dost wisdom learn
Then bless the tempest which thy shipwreck brought.
Is death no blessing to blind man who errs
While on his trial in his mortal frame?
So strong is nature's witchcraft o'er mankind
That sovereign reason must to instinct yield,
And souls are dreading the ethereal space
To breathe the dust of this heart-writhing world.
There seems none greater than the crowned head,
And what hath he for all the cares of rule?
That sweetest third of life we spend in sleep
Is more the peasant's than the king's repose,
Who rests uneasy by those phantoms scared
Which haunt his mind in fullest glare of day.
And bread and salt, the beggar's relished fare
Than royal dainties sweeter are to health,
To hearts unworried and to conscience pure.
But worse than all to crowned heads is death,
Whose terrors grow compared with royal pomp.
How foolish they who, born without their choice,
Would have a will when it is time to part,
As if the pleasures tasted here below
The highest were a universe provides
For such as do in virtuous deeds delight.
   Ant. Speak not of virtue, at whose sight I sneered,
Browbeating her with power's haughty front.
But shame and evil crowd upon my soul
That must be torn from this decaying flesh;
And when the deeps unfathomable of the
Hereafter I affrighted pierce, I curse
The hour in which I was conceived to wreck
So many ere I wrecked myself. Sprung from
A royal ancestry of noblest blood,
The savage Parthian I in crime did match,
And have no courage mercy to implore
Of Him whose image I in man disdained.
How can a second of repentance forced
Efface the trail of crimeful, bloody years?
   Mana. Commit no sin, my prince, in doubting that
The greatest God the greatest is in grace,
Else how could frail mankind one hour subsist
With all the errors they with air inhale?

Or wouldst thou Deity with man compare,
Who sets a limit to his mortal love,
And wreaks his vengeance on a sinking foe?
No, for thy shortcomings thine death atones,
And clears of guilt thy sin-encumbered soul.
By deep remorse do sanctify this hour
And to thy ghost upsoaring virtue give
By rueing earnestly thy dark career.
Above thy lower instincts rise, dear prince,
And with a bosom filled with heavenly trust,
A temper softened by contrition's flow,
Embrace the moment with a man's resolve
And part resigned to the decree of Heaven!
    Ant. Oh, if my career on earth had been as pure
As my repentance now is true and deep,
I would an angel not a sinner die.
Yea, night, eternal night I do embrace,
And may in darkness buried rest my shame;
Come, headsman, come and cut my earthly race,
That I thus fall none but myself I blame.
                    [*He leaves followed by Manahem and the Headsman.*

ACT II.

SCENE I.

A hall in the palace.

HEROD, MARIAMNE, ALEXANDRA, ARISTOBULUS *in priestly attire,*
PHERORAS, DIOPHANTUS, SARAMELLAS, EURYCLES, JOSEPH *and*
CORINTHUS.

Herod. Now seems all joy and brightness in our mid
And you, our queen, are shining like the sun
In his mild glories of the morrow wrapt,
And we are brightening at your radiant smile.
What is a throne devoid of loveliness,
A world of wealth without a blessed saint!
More than the beggar feels the want of bread
The careworn sovereign needs the charm of love
To sweeten soothingly his restless days.
That smile to chain we would a treasure give
Could by some magic we arrest its beam,
Since having it our day would never end —
And you, our mother, are not less enjoyed
As if your heart no ardent wish enclosed.
Yet if a longing slumbers in your breast
Which we, perchance, are slow to satisfy
This hour be yours; demand, we grant,
And let no sigh becloud this festive day.
    Alex. So satiate of the moment's joy is mind
And heart in me, my king, that for a wish
There is scarce room in them, except the one
That what I see and have may ever last!
Mattathias' immortal offsprings for

The purple fought my son as high priest hath
A claim to wear, for in his veins the blood
Of Maccabæus, Simon and Jonathan flows
Who for Judea's freedom striving fell.
Yet is by Heaven's will the power thine,
And I am thankful for my daughter's share
Of the inheritance endeared to us,
Am thankful that my sire's office filled
Is by mine son. Henceforth no thought of mine
Shall wrong thee, king; and if, thy unrevealed
Designs mistaking, I oft rued thy course,
Forgive, my lord, a mother's throbbing heart
Who for her children would herself consume.—
And now a favor grant, my lord, and share
The banquet I in Jericho, my son's
Promotion duly to acknowledge, have
Ordained. May none who friend is of thy throne
Be absent from the joyous feast I give.
    Her. We rate it highly to be named your guest,
And shall our court command to honor you
In all particulars of royal state.
We owe you much for our beloved queen
Who to our bosom dearer is than thrones,
And do our best to stimulate her love
And have your friendship and esteem withal.—
There comes the hoary sire whom we revere,
By us invited to endow the youth

    Enter HYRCANUS *and train—all incline their heads*

With all the symbols of the sacred rank.—
Come, father, and thy grandson raise to that
Distinction which thy life adorned. Invest
Aristobulus with the high priest's awe.
Be he the minister of the Great One
And on this Harvest Feast let him the skies
For us and human kind beseech.
    Hyr. [*his hand on Aristobulus' head*] My son,
The truth from Sinai's height to Israel
Revealed engrave upon thy tender heart
And by it led thy sacred calling fill.
Thou art the teacher of a princely race
Ordained to save the erring tribes of man,
And on thy lip this nation's weal depends.
Thy station bids thee soar above this world,
Confront corruption with a manly breast
And purge of errors straying multitudes.
Unlike the heathen priests who sway the crowds
By superstitious practice, false pretense,
Judea's priesthood claims the sacrifice
Of those who vow its banner to uphold
With all the manhood sacred truth involves!
Thou all sublunar passions must forswear
Except the worship of the awful One,
With glowing ardor thrilling every soul,
And virtue tested by the tongue of deeds.—
This oil I pour upon thy youthful locks
                .   [*pouring oil on his head.*

Transfers on thee a people's holiest trust,
And opes the Sanctuary's fearful Shrine
Where thou shalt pray for Israel and man.—
And thou Supremest of all beings high,
His prayers hear whenever he invokes
Thy boundless grace for them who living err;
And may through him this country thriving grow,
This monarch's reign be one of lasting peace!
   Her. And our felicitation, brother, take,   ′
Who from our heart bestow on thee the rank.
The sky beseech that we may prosper well
In what abroad we foster or at home,
And teach the tribes to venerate their king
Whom Heaven chose this country to redeem
From foreign bondage and intestine strife.
We stand determined for the land's repute
And shall its prestige jealously maintain
If not disturbed by unsubmissive mobs,
Whom thou as teacher timely must exhort
And spare us bloodshed in defence of peace.
   Arist. Could I my soul's emotion on the tongue
Uplift, and utterance impart to what
I thrilling feel, no eye is here but would
With sympathy for my affrighted youth
Pathetically melt and overflow.—
Must I in wisdom poorer than in years,
And in the latter wanting to a score
Approach invokingly the Lord of Hosts,
A mediator stand betwixt the heavens
And earth! The wisest heads whom learned age
Adorned, struck with the dreadful sacredness
Of Him who in the Holi▸st of Holies dwells,
When on the great Atonement Day they yon
Sequestered space bestrode, their terror of
Jehovah's breath much stronger found than life,
And I should face that all-enkindling blaze
With thousand follies boyhood hath in train!   [*He kneels.*
Oh Lord Zebaoth who my fathers braced
When with bare sword Judea's foes they faced
And fell devoted to Thy sacred word,
Hear when I pray and what I pray accord!
Let me be worthy of Thy holy trust
And serve thee faithful, ardent to the last.
This realm may prosper in its blessed clime,
This nation triumph as in Solomon's time!

   [*He rises; Alexandra and Mariamne kiss him, Herod and
      Hyrcanus congratulate, the others bow in reverence; while
      the king, the queen, Alexandra, Hyrcanus and trains depart
      Pheroras beckons Eurycles to stay.*]

   Pher. Well, friend, how look these things to one from Greece?
   Eury. Not worse than to the fool from Palestine.
A priest, a cloak, a blessing and a talk
Leave me as frigid as a frozen fish;
But for the queenly kiss I barefoot ran
On Hades' coal. She beats the heroine
Of Troy, and I a hundred Hectors would

For her encounter.   Zounds, Herod hath a cause
To live and strive; for with a grace like this
What treasures has the earth that are not his?

Pher. Thou art a Greek of Helen's native soil,
And strains like this are common in your land;
But if thou ever art of Herod's suite
Avoid to give such sentiments a sound
Lest fortune flees thee by mine brother's side.

Eury. He would not others hear his wealth compute?

Pher. He would his eunuchs' impotence not trust
And loves not him who wondering eyes his queen.

Eury Saturnia, perhaps gave Herod birth;
His jealousy is worthy of her brood.—
I am no eyeless eunuch, prince, and will
My suit to serve Judea's king retract.

Pher. Is silence galling to a man of wit?
Success will follow him who can be mute.
Is woman's weakness not her tongue's defect,
And manhood's strength not full control of speech?

Eury. I stand instructed, prince, and will comply
If I be welcome to the wondrous king.

Pher. The wondrous king dislikes not wondrous men
Who, like thyself, come with their fortunes to
Enhance their wondrous luck. But lucre not,
Good man, will pave to Herod's confidence
Thy way.   The servants he selects must be
Of mettle other than the vulgar type.

Eury. By thundering Jove, I am the flesh he wants,
My sole ambition being to unearth
Unruly rascals and betray abuse!
As all of us can neither monarchs be
Nor lords, nor otherwise of dazzling note,
The best of means to conquer some repute
Is to connect one's fate with those who reign
And be promoter of their higher ends.
What are we if no factors in the whirl
Of life! Let woman cry for rest, but man
In stirring action seeks and finds his poise.
I thirst for deeds, and hope the field is found
Or I have vainly left my slothful home
In search of emprise nowhere to be had.
It is a crawling age in which we live,
My prince, and all the world would snore but for
The Roman who the bustle stirs.

Pher.   We in
This quarter have some pith as well and in
The king thou wilt a temper find who would
In naught to any Roman yield.   First know
The man whom Antony an equal deems
In pluck to conquer and in craft to rule.
Think not so lightly of our valor, friend,
By Rome acknowledged and by facts sustained.

Eury. Your wide renown drew hither me, my lord,
And manly pride incites to serve the great.
The Spartan learned Herod to extol
And thinks it station to be among his train.
But this is more, it seems, than I deserve,

Who thus presumptuously would rank attain.
Nay, better I withdraw and go my way
Than cringe a suppliant at this famous court.
Why not abide in mute obscurity,
Instead of craving such an envious lot
As few can get devoid of titled names?
   Pher. Mistake, mistake! Be not too humble, man,
And give no preference to a scurvy stock
Of rotten softlings o'er a breed of steel.
This time the vulgars in their clutches hold
The world, and they of royal lineage may
The vapors smell of what the upstarts feast,
But lack in nerve the booty to dispute.
Thy vulgar origin commends thee well,
And I will prompt the king to have thee nigh.
Be not afar should I thy presence want.
Meanwhile be student of all men and things
And let no striking incident thy watch
Elude.--Be near when from the Shrine the king
And court return, and scent the current of
The rabble's views.—Be near, I shall somehow
Requite thy costly gifts.
   Eury.   My prince—
   Pher.   No word!
Be near at Jericho.   [*Exit Pheroras.*
   Eury.   I shall be near,
So near that of thy shadow my Greek nose
Shall make a part. It is a risk to give
So much away to buy admission to
A quivering throne and be the creature of
An upstart rogue. But in this hunting world
Thou canst unhazardously not a rat
Or hare entrap. If I in Herod am
Deceived and find him wiser, better than
A cunning knave, a man by consciousness
And usages controlled, my prospects fade
And I my wreckage have too dearly bought.
But what of him I know by hearsay tends
To prove that he much bolder is in act
Than in his wisdom deep, and that his creed
Is pliant as his mind. Love softens him;
Ambition and suspicion haunt his rest
And magnify the spectres of his fear.
How easy to confound a man like this!
So much I know that he his wife adores
But would her stock exterminate at once
Had he a shade of ground to justify
The crime. He wants a rogue of such a type
As I am through and through, just made to fill
The vacancy. Be it, however, known
To these unspeaking walls that not for love
To Herod do his confidence I seek,
But hunt my interest in hunting him.
I may be lamb or tiger in this frame,
It all depends upon the means I need
To get what I much higher rate than fame;
The devil's lucre is my Grecian creed.   [*Exit.*

SCENE II.

A room in the palace.

Enter CYPROS *and* SALOME.

Cypros. Let her upon her rotten lineage perch,
My tree is young and vigorous, and can
Her slurs defy. Enough my son is king
Against her kindred and her own consent,
And she may plume herself to have his love.

Sal. His love and what a monarch thus enslaved
May to his arrogant enchantress give.
What can a woman not who knows her might!
Mariamne knows that Herod is her slave,
And would his power forfeit rather than
Her lukewarm love. I wonder not that he
A sister's tenderness but slightly notes,
But loathe is every filial sense in me
When I his wife above his mother in
Superior loftiness exalted see.
Oh fie, to be so great and yet so weak!

Cyp. It is no weakness in a man to love,
Though weak it is to love beyond degree.
His father likewise was a burning type
Yet knew he measure in his glowing heat,
And I ofttimes in vain have tried to move
Him off a scheme on which his heart was set.
In every feature Herod is his like,
In manly hardiness, tempestuous wrath,
In crafty projects puzzling friend and foe.
Uxoriousness cannot his dotage be,
And if it be it surely hath a bound.

Sal. If I judge well he loves but is not loved,
Or those he honors she would honor too,
Instead of treating us with marked contempt.

Cyp. Contempt! no, say not this. Mariamne shows
No liking for us all, 'tis true, but naught
I know of proves the feeling thou didst name.

Sal. That means she did not spit at us when we
In homage bowed before her queenly grace,
While she did graciously our fealty by
A nod return, sometimes a smile so forced
That words but little to the scorn could add.
What could she do she did not to abate
Our pride? Once I of father's greatness spoke.
"Yes, great through him who greater is than he."
Alluding to Hyrcanus this she said.
And when of Herod's matchless valor I
Dilating spoke, she asked me sneeringly
If I thought Judas Maccabæus was
As brave as he, withdrawing ere I time
Had to reply. Such haughty ways the best
Of natures must envenomingly wound.   [*Enter Pherorus.*
I hate that woman whom I long to sting.

Cyp. What brings my son beside himself to-day?

Pher. If aught I bring it more weighs than myself,
Who but for stomachs which give fools some weight
Would be too light to walk against the wind.

Sal. Thy dagger makes thee ponderous for thy foes
Who by a breath would blow thee off the earth.
    Pher. Let daggers, sister, in their scabbards rust
Now that the black-eyed maidens garlands weave
And every pathway strewed is with sweet flowers.
From all the corners of Judea's reach
The joyous crowds come streaming to the Shrine
The Feast of Harvest duly to observe,
To hear the high priest's tuneful clarion voice,
To kiss his purple's border, shed a tear,
Receive his new-hatched blessing, see the queen,
And then on blessing, beauty, high priest, king,
Oppression, tyranny descant at home.
But we have something more—a feast, a feast,
A banquet at the mansion of the dame
In Jericho, who overjoyed with her
Endeared heir's advancement, king and court
Invites to honor him now worshipped by
The mob. You will, of course, be with us there
To-night. I guess there will be fun for you.
    Cyp. Would not frail age my absence justify?
I am too old for feasts and frolic sports.
    Pher. Command thy son who will thy age excuse.—
But thou, Salome, bear us company;
The king would miss thee and the court withal;
Among the fairs there should be one of us.
    Sal. I hate to meet the overbearing queen
Who in imperious insolence her dam
Excels. Yet not to fly her sight I am
Resolved, but with my valiant brothers shall
My place maintain. I am a princess as
She is a queen, nor was my father less
A man than hers.—I shall the feast attend
Which may for them in doleful sorrow end.   [*Exit.*
    Pher. A red-hot fury this and gentle vow.—
What, by Azazel, means this pitchy rage?
    Cyp. The queen's demeanor stings one to the quick
And naught is done to damp her haughtiness.
We have good reasons to resent her slurs.
    Pher. Did her Mariamne offer blunt offense?
    Cyp. As blunt as faces, words and acts betray.
Thou knowest well she liketh not our house.
    Pher. Not more nor less than we her kindred like;
Yet should it never come to open war
Until by force and guile we one by one
Remove. Vivacious is her withering stock
We must by inches extirpate; but spoil
Our method not by such unmeasured shows.
    Cyp. Is not Hyrcanus still in power high,
Aristobulus not the priest of state?
You nurse the hydra which in morsels cut
Would out of every piece conjure a snake.
I see no wisdom in your method, boys.
    Pher. If hydra heads would each a hydra turn
We torches had each hydra's head to burn.
Events will speak, thus let me silent be
And mutely ripen our sure victory. [*Exeunt Pheroras and Cypros.*

SCENE III.

Before the Temple.

Enter SABION, ÆSOP, *and a crowd all bearing branches of palm
trees and boughs of myrtle.*

Æsop. Oh Sabion, friend, dear Sabion, why not weep!
Not weep with joy! I am a woman, faith,
But who, beholding that imperial youth
In purple clad and towering over all
The pious throngs, could muster his delight?
I wept, all wept, while he did minister.
Didst thou the king observe? Dejected, eh?
Dejected; paled he not?
   Sab.   Be not so loud,
The people there have ears, and when the king
Is named they listen eagerly.—Well, friends,
This palm and myrtle show will haunt you far,
And furnish rich material for a tale
To be recounted at your distant homes.
Our high priest's blessing light on you, good men! [*To the crowd.*
   Æsop. Ho, friends, God bless our youthful priest! Send up
Your prayers for the lordly youth in whom
This land and people may be fully blessed!
          Enter another crowd. A voice is heard.
Revere the high priest coming from the Shrine!
[*Herod and suite, Hyrcanus, Aristobulus in holy vesture issue
   from the Temple's portal. At seeing Aristobulus all
      incline their heads and the multitude exclaims:*|
Long live Aristobulus, our high priest!
   A Voice. A cheer for Hyrcanus, a cheer for Hyrcanus, ho!
   Crowd. Hail King Hyrcanus, pray for King Hyrcanus!
   A Voice. Five cheers for Herod, five cheers for Herod, ho!
(*The crowd grows tumultuous; coughing, laughing and sneezing
   are heard while the train passes by, the king being visibly
   affected.*)
   A Voice. A groan, a groan!—
   Another Voice. A cough, a kick, and a groan! [*Loud laughter.*
   Æsop. Hear me, ye sons of Judea, hear me and do
What I, the servant of our princess, say.
   A Citizen. Hear him, hear Æsop, silence, ho, hear him!
   Another Cit. Friends, lend this man an ear who bears some news
With him; he is the faithful servant of——
   Another Cit. Shut up, we know, we hear him!—Speak, Æsop—
The news, what are the news thou hast, we hear.
   Æsop. Our high priest's mother, Alexandra, our
Fair princess, celebrates the coming eve
At Jericho her son's promotion by
A sumptuous feast, to which you all, who may
Before this day's decline, that city reach,
Are welcome, welcome rich and poor! A cheer
For the princess, ho! a cheer for the princess!
   Crowd. Hail princess! Long live the princess. [*Exit crowd.*
   Sab.   What more
Can Alexandra wish now that her son
The longed-for furtherance secured? He is
A brilliant youth, and she may weep with joy.

Æsop. Oh, she was sighing for this blessed day,
And may no cloud her sunny visions dim.—
The king was pale and bit his under lip
When him the roaring mass would not, as king
Salute, while they Hyrcanus and the youth
Rejoicingly did hail.—How may things end?
Sab. How may things end?
Æsop.   Yes, Sabion, I have thoughts
So odd that I would fain be called a fool.
Sab. What are thy thoughts?
Æsop.   My thoughts?
Sab.   Ay, let me hear
Thy thoughts; perchance we guess and fear the same.
Æsop. I fear the worst, and guess that schemes are ripe
Against the Asmoneans.—I hit thy guess?
Sab. Humph—
Æsop.   Humph, well, I wish thou couldst convince me that
I am a fool.—There is no amity
Betwixt the princess and the king, who did
Against his will the youth promote, and that
Acclaim the king makes jealous of the prince.
The princess still on Cleopatra counts,
And through Antonius' mistress much can do.
Aristobulus would not minister
Had Egypt through that Roman not prevailed
To put the mitre where it justly rests.
Sab. What could this happy state of things upset,
Aristobulus being in his place?
Æsop. As was Ananelus ejected though
In violation of our sacred Law.
There is a tempest brewing in the air,
I smell it, Sabion, smell it and I pray
That He in Heaven's shield the guiltless heads.—
Enough of this, it softens me to tears.—
Thou wilt to Jericho with me proceed
There tankards huge are filled for thee and all.—
I prattle forth when I should be where I
Am wanted most.—Wilt thou to Jericho?
Sab. Go on thy way, my horse will bring me there
In time. I have some business here to do.
Æsop. Thou must not disappoint the princess, man,
Who would in thee a loyal countenance miss.
Sab. I shall be there if I be yet alive.
Æsop. Come not too late and bring what friends thou hast.
Why, it is sultry to be sure to-day.
Sab. It is a glowing noon. Farewell. I must
Return and see my folks at home.
Æsop.   Farewell. [*Exit Æsop.*
Sab. That honest prattler bears his heart upon
His tongue, and sees what every one-eyed man
Can dreaming see. Proud Alexandra on my
Adherence counts which makes the monarch hate
Me in extreme. He bears me rancor since
By mine device, he knows too well, the shrewd
Antipater was murderously slain.
It is a risky game I play, but I
Must try to make the king believe I am

His friend by keeping him apprised of what
Concerning Alexandra's moves I know.—
Thy cause is lost, my princess, thus forgive
That on thy downfall I attempt to live.　　　　　　*[Exit.*

SCENE IV.

*Jericho. Night. A garden before Alexandra's mansion all
illuminated. Noise and music heard.*

Enter EURYCLES.

Eurycles. So am since hours I hanging, like a wolf
About a stinking carcass, round this house,
And wrapt in dusky twilight I did many
A secret overhear which clearly show
Some tapers here mean gory work to-night.
I could not well connect the purport of
The whispered talk except that drowning in
A fish-pond is the meditated sport,
And this while swimming in a playful mood.
Who is the cub to get the dip I have
To guess.—Hush, another pair come to consult
In dark. I must withdraw just far enough
To catch the substance of the low discourse.
　　　　(*He withdraws.* PHERORAS *and* PHABATUS *Enter*).
Pher. Now mark me well, the new-fledged priest must go,
Be drowned in sport, of course, to suffocate
Suspicion 'gainst the king and court. He must
Be dipped, Phabatus, or the work of years
Is lost. It is an act of self-defense.
Phab. I have the parties trained for the affair.
Once in the wave he never shall return;
The Galls will dip him till his breath is out.
But how to get him there, that is the pinch.
Pher. Let me take care of this. I have a means
Concocted with the king to tempt him there,
When thou must do the rest if thou art man
Enough thy furtherance to effect. It is
A bidding which a favor can be deemed.
Phab. Rely on me the moment he is there.
　　　　　　　　　　　　　　[The king comes forth.
He shall be drowned or I will drown myself.
Pher. I see the king who likely seeks for me.—
Go hold in readiness thy valiant band.　　　*[Exit Phabatus.*
Eury. [*emerging*] I will accost him now; but lo! the king!
Well, be it so, I still approach the prince.—　*[Stepping forth.*
Dear lord, excuse an uninvited guest,
But thee obeying I did follow here.
Her. [*drawing near Pheroras*] Who is that man emerging from
　　　the dark?
Pher. He took me by surprise, I do profess,
But own he is a man I like, a Greek,
A wary Spartan who the king would serve,
And bids a fortune to repay the right
Of being one of thy devoted suite.　　*[Cheers and music heard.*
Her. What canst thou do a common rogue could not?
Eury. I can my lord's intention make the mine,
His purpose serve at cost of limb and life,

His secrets bury in my faithful breast,
Unfolding such as I can steal of foes.
There is no task I shun a man can do.
   Her. Of all the Grecian creeds the which is thine?
   Eury. That one by which I best can thrive below.
I trust a feast is better than a fast,
That he who dares not run will come the last,
That five is more than four, and three than two.
That what is best for me I sure must do.
   Her. Thou art of Satan's most tenacious boys,
I see, and canst do useful work in my
Employ. The Greeks are great in every sense.—
Is he not privy to our dark design?   [*To Pheroras.*
   Pher. Not that I know, unless he heard me to
Phabatus speak.   [*Looking at Eurycles.*
   Eury.   I heard or heard not, just
As you would have me framed.
   Her.   Thy fortune we
Decline, but do thy service readily
Accept. Acquaint him, prince, with our intents
To-night, and let the others welcome him
As guest.—Suggest the garden for a cool
Disport. The air is close and they are all
Intoxicate with merriment and wine.
[*Pheroras and Eurycles enter the house, whence noise, cheers
    and music issue all the time.*]
   Her. So must it be or I am soon undone,
The people treat me not as monarch, whilst
The priestly grandchild and his grandsire live.
Thou first, my boy, and then the old out of
My path must come. Pah, conscience, conscience, when
One sees that nature none hath in her course.
What is there is and that is all that is.
There is necessity and force. That kind
Which strongest is in mould survives the rest.
There is no conscience in great nature's realms!
It is the bugaboo by woman nursed
And superstitious priests, as if not on
The fly the spider, and on both the bird
Doth feed, as on the lamb the wolf, and on
The harmless beast mankind. But man!—Yea, man
With soul, with reason, conscience, choice; the lord
Of earth, and Heaven's image—man should be—what?
Divine! infallible, perfect, like—like whom?
Well here we stop.—Like whom? The story tells
What saints they were who taught us to be good.
See father Abraham his concubine
And babe, to please her jealous mistress, drive
To dreary wilderness with bread and water
For a day. See cunning Jacob Esau's rights
Appropriating by a rogish trick;
His saintly sons enslave their flesh and blood.
See Moses murder in a fit of rage,
Aaron shape an idol for the mob.
Why speak of David who the husband slays
To hide the lechery of adulterous sheets!
Why name his darling whose death he bewails,

After the chase the son his father gave!
A goodly multitude of saints these are
To whom compared I am, of course, profane;
Nay, too profane to rule this godly race!
I am not of the Asmonean's blood,
And as in clipping brother's ears I can
Antigonus not match, I shall confine
Myself to clipping heads and drowning those
I like not in my way.—When thou art still,
Hyrcanus, no Endor's Witch thy slumber shall
Disturb. But there is time for thee, old man;
Thy fledgeling must be first enskied, and thou
Shalt follow him.—The doors are opening wide;
The guests must not behold me here alone.   [*Exit.*
[*Servants bearing torches open the doors. The Queen, Alexan-
    dra, Salome, and other ladies followed by Hyrcanus, Aristob·
    ulus, Pheroras, Diophantus, Saramellas, Joseph, Phabatus,
    Corinthus, Eurycles, Sabion, and Æsop come forth.*]
    Æsop. More lights! Illumine the groves, ho, more lights!—
The groves are cool, delicious cool. The prince
Is right, the air beneath the roof is hot,
Sultry, fearful, fearful.—Bring lights, more lights!
[*The ladies attended lose themselves in the next grove.*]
    Pher. Who leads us to the coolest spot? A breeze,
A breeze is worth a million at this hour.
Where are your basins, Æsop? Lead us where
Some waters flow. I own that in mine eyes
The happiest of creatures is the fish.
    Arist. Come prince, my lords come on, I lead you where
The finny denizens in cool disport.
Our spacious gardens will your want supply.—
See that the fish-ponds be by torches lit.— [*To Æsop who leaves.*
Where is the king? I miss the king!
    Phab.   The king,
Sweet prince, within these pleasure-grounds somewhere
Sojourns, he having found the walls too close
Before our perspiration forced us to
Desert the wines. Our noise will draw him near.
    Hyr. Dear friends, I feel my limbs are weaker than
My will. Oppressive age is mounted on
My back, to whom submitting I must seek
A spot to rest my head. Be joyous, friends,
Without my useless company. The wine,
The humid air and noise assail my nerves.
The gracious Lord protect you all. Good night.
    All. Good night, dear sir.   [*Some kiss his hand.*
    Æsop. [*who re-entered*] Come, holy sire. I will
Thy rooms unlock and to thy comfort see. [*Exit with Hyrcanus.*
    Arist. Now after me who longs to drink the breeze. [*Exeunt all.*

SCENE V.

A place in the garden.

Enter HEROD *and* SABION.

Her. That she no friendly feeling nursed for us
We knew it well, but hoped that change of things

Would in her bosom work an equal change.
Her son's promotion ought to sate her pride.
What could we do we have not done for her
Whose vows and smiles, 'tis clear, we cannot trust?
Still scheming, raging 'gainst her daughter's lord!
What are the grievances she may advance?
   Sab. I know not all, save that she fears thou art
Not true to her, and wouldst exterminate
The Asmonean stock, and this to Egypt she
Impugning wrote, imploring aid against
Thy tameless cruelty; which knowing I
Felt bound thee of her doings to apprise,
Expecting it might some calamity
Avert, and clearly prove that Sabion is
Not hostile to thy beneficial sway.
Some idle tongues, I know, by false reports
Upon my head have put a heavy guilt
Which to disprove I ever sought a chance.
   Her. Disprove not what no man could ever prove,
Or Sabion would not thus to Herod speak.
Our father's death by Malichus was planned,
And thou art guiltless of the heinous crime
Avenged by us on the assassin's head.
But wilt thou truly be our trusty friend?
   Sab. If Herod doubts why should him Sabion serve
Before conviction takes suspicion's place?
I will be neutral in this land's affair.
The hand is strong that yields the helm of state,
And time will show that Sabion means it well.
   Her. Thy honored age and wisdom we require
And thy impatience in thy favor pleads.
We make thee partner of our great resolves,
And will, henceforth, behold in thee a friend
With all the claims of confidential trust.
Keep us informed of all weighty steps
And be assured we bear thee in our mind.—   *[Exit Sabion.*
This treacherous move thy nature's bent betrays,
And Antipater's voice I hear exclaim :
"That murderous knave did help to cut me off !"
I make thee spy before to hell thy ghost
I send.—That woman smells my purpose, and
The Roman's harlot on the Nile I hate!—   *[Enter Aristobulus.*
There comes the bird I plumed for Pluto's pit
As Druids plume their beasts for slaughter marked.—
Alone, my boy, without a girl to hug!
In search of whom didst thou the revellers fly?
   Arist. In search of him I do as father love.   *[Kisses Herod.*
Oh dear, Jonathan loved not David more
Than I my sister's royal consort love.
Thy absence tells me what in thee I have,
And, missing thee, I felt so lonesome, soft,
And overcome of indefinable pangs
That weeping only could relieve my heart.
What is it, dear, that makes me sad to-night?
   Herod. A whim, a sentimental whim, my boy.
What else? Is all not to thy liking now?   *[Taking his hand.*

Look here, my boy, thy love is well bestowed
On one who would a crown set on thy head.
　Arist. Oh no, no dear, no crown; I would I wore
The mitre not which weighs me down. It is
An awful thing to be a minister
Of the Most High, and meditating stand
Betwixt the skies and man. Remembering
The dreadful One to whom for Israel
I prayed and thine triumphal rule, methought,
The Sanctuary was ablaze with light
Of seraphim my fancy eyed around,
—Celestial sprights our prophets often see—
I trembling stood upon the altar's ground,
Scarce heard the Levites' song nor trumpet's sound,
Then sank and prayed upon my bended knee.
　Herod. Thy mood, my darling prince, affects my heart
And is no temper for a merry feast.
Come, child, and let no senseless notion take
Possession of thy unbeclouded youth.
Why, why, thou art the cause and host of this
Event, and wouldst thy guests have dance with thee
And weep? These things go ill together, dear.
If thou a longing hast to see me weep,
I am wrought up to woman's softness at
Thy touch.—The air in this environment
Appears prophetic or the gods betray
The webs invisible of mortal brains.　　　　　　　　*[Aside*
　Arist. What didst thou mutter just I did not hear?
　Her. I muttered at the heat which spares no king.
Is not a cooler place around us here?
　Arist. Why, yes, my dear, as cool as when the heavens
Their blessed showers pour on earth. Am I
Not selfish thus thy joyance to abate
With thoughts unhealthy as the vapor of
A swampy land? Thou dost not think me drunk?
　Her. I would the wine had spoken what thou saidst.
I know not why thy humor works on me
　Arist. I emptied many a goblet to thy health
But could the morbid sentiments not force
Out of my breast.
　Her.　　　　　I banish them straightway.
Come let us wager. He who fleeter runs
Shall of Judea have the fleetest steed
As price. No talk, no talk, a word, a bet!
I swim in perspiration, thou will win.
　Arist. Agreed! save one condition I impose.
　Her. I should not faster run than thou?
　Arist.　　　　　　　　　　　　Not let
Me winner be without a racing test.
We start, thou fourteen feet ahead of me,
And if I touch thee with my outstretched hand
I claim the steed.
　Her.　　　　　The steed be thine if I
Within thy touch come ere we reach the pond.
But knowest thou that I with Bedouins fought,
Who are the fleetest of the desert's tribes,
Yet ever overtook the foe I chased?

Arist. If this be so, then loss cannot disgrace
Me should I lack in speed, while thy defeat
My triumph to myself would mar. I would
My vanity at thy expense not feed.
   Her. I risk my fame in this.—Well, fourteen feet?
   Arist. Yes, measure fourteen feet and then we start.
[*Herod measvres fourteen feet, counting one, two, three; they*
   run toward the grove.]

SCENE VI.

Before a fish-pond.

PHERORAS *and the guests of the court. Some are bathing afar;*
torches burning.

   Pheroras. Haste on, boys, haste; there in the groves undress;
With water mix you wine-benumbed heads.
I join you soon, it is a healthful sport.—
Undress, undress, I see them yonder, come.
[*Aside to Eurycles who withdraws.*

Enter HEROD *closely followed by* ARISTOBULUS *who overtakes him.*

   Arist. The steed, Judea's fleetest steed is mine!
   Pher. It must be fleet indeed thee to outrun,
My prince.—The king is out of breath and beaten!
   Her. And not without resistance, to be sure.
If prince Aristobulus speed in all
As well as in his feet, he'll beat the world.
   Pher. Look how the boys are sporting in the waves.
There seems delight to bathe in torchlight's gleam.
   Her. I am disposed to partake of the sport
And try in water to regain what I
By land have lost.—Who is that fellow there
Who like a seal the billows cuts in twain?
   Pher. It is the Spartan who did challenge all
To match his quickness in the swimming art;
He bids a fortune none is prone to get.
   Arist. Were it a fitting wager I would dare
To cope with him in skill, but would not with
A heathen for a prize engage. With one
Of you I gladly would the pond divide.
And either forfeit what I racing won
Or double it should victory be mine. [*Enter Æsop.*
   Her. Stood I not beaten thus and sweating I
Once more would stake my reputation and
Another steed. But now, Pheroras, thou
The challenge take, or I will think a pike
Can more accomplish than a valiant prince.
   Pher. I take the challenge, prince.
 Æsop. [*to Aristobulus*]   My lord, my prince,
Night is no time for such a risky play.
Good princes, for your sake I do beseech,
Postpone the competition, 'tis too late.
   Pher. Shall we postpone it for some other hour?
I fear no darkness when the torches burn.
   Arist. I go ahead if thou wilt follow me.
   Pher. I follow thee, although I lose the game. |*They leave.*

Her. [to *Æsop*] You let us know who of the two did win.
We to the ladies must repair, whom we
Ungallantly too long forsook to-night.
Where is the queen and mother at this hour?
Æsop. They from the night's humidity in the
Saloon which fronts this garden refuge sought,
My lord. Shall I accompany the king?
 Her. No need of this; the path is known to us. [*Exit Herod.*
 Æsop. Oh, Lord forgive if I suspect these men
Whose outward seldom mirrors what they are.—
I hear them plunge, but see them not; my sight
Is dim and torches dazzle me. But hark! [*Voices heard afar.*
Voices and laughter.—Sabion is not there,
Not one among the throng on whom to count
Should anything the darling youth befall.
 A Voice. [*from afar*] No life in him! he sinks, is drowned—dead!
 Æsop. What was it? Dead! Drowned! The echo of
My voice I fear, so rings the bittern's wail
In dead of night.—My prince, what happened?—Lord!
 Pher. [*who enters half dressed*] Go, run, the king, the queen,
  —call doctors here.—
There might be help yet.—Run, the prince is drowned!
 Æsop. Drowned, the prince! What prince, the high priest, no?
 Pher. They say he breathes yet; yonder in the grove
They try him to reanimate.—Be gone!
 Æsop. Thou gracious Power, Sovereign of the skies,
Thy will be done, but I am loath to live.—
My prince, my gentle prince, oh sacred child!
Ah, ah, ah, drowned, drowned, drowned,—dead!   [*Exit.*
 Pher. [*enter Phabatus and Eurycles*] That pious beast annoys
  me with his looks.
That godly ass perchance may smell the truth
And with his brays upstir the kicking herd.—
You did your duty, boys, but it behooves
Us to misguide suspicion off our track.
Come let us overtake that howling clown
And mix our wailing with his assish cries.
That patch of piety defies all bribes,
And for his mistress and her cub would die.   [*Exeunt all.*

SCENE VII.

A saloon.

The king, the queen, ALEXANDRA, SALOME, *and attendance.*

Herod. Yes, we are beaten, ladies, hoping though
It will your measure of our valor not
Affect. We did our best, but strove in vain.
All Greece would smile to see a high priest and
A monarch run a race, but we are glad
That few did witness our ungraced defeat.
 Mari. I fear the king was willing to award
The prize else not an Arab could outwing
My lord. I am not sorry Herod lost
The game, knowing the joy the steed will bring
To him.

Alex. He is not one at trifles to
Rejoice. I find him older since in rank
He rose. He thinks the sacred calling more
Than he deserves, so humble, modest is
My dearest son. Yet lacks he not in nerve
When manly enterprise provokes, and, like
His glorious ancestors, could calmly face
A host of armed foes, but is a lamb
In innocence when charmed by a smile.— [*Æsop enters weeping.*
Why, Æsop, weeping! Æsop—thy speech—thy speech!—
Æsop. Thou wilt henceforth the tiger's growl prefer
To my despair-impregnate speech to-day.—
My speech is death!—death, princess, is my speech!
Ah, ah, ah, drowned, my gentle prince, drowned——
All. [*startled*] Who drowned?——
Her.   What prince? How drowned?
Mari. Speak fool!—
Æsop. [*weeping*] Ah, ah, my princess, thy son—drowned—dead.
                                        [*To Alexandra.*
Alex. My son! my boy, my high priest, drowned—dead!
Ha, ha, ha, ha, ha, ha, ha, ha!—Go to,
Gray devil—nay, dear Æsop—deny it—ha!
My son, Aristobulus, drowned, dead?
            Enter PHERORAS, PHABATUS, *and* EURYCLES.
Æsop. [*as before*] Dead, dead thy son—forever dead—dead—
            dead.—
They saw him, they know it all—dead, forever dead.—
                                        [*Fearful pause.*
Alex. Thy dark decrees are fearful, dreadful Lord!
Now darken, sun, I hate to see thy light!
My boy, my boy, my son, O, O, O! mute,
Forever mute thy lips that ministered
To-day to twenty myriad throbbing hearts!—
Oh daughter, daughter, dead, thy brother dead! [*To Mariamne.*
My heir, my darling drowned in the flood
And all is blackness.—Oh my wits, my wits
Are turning!—Graces, powers, heavens, where is
My dearest, sweetest, gentlest, godliest child!—
                        [*Exit Alexandra followed by some ladies.*
Mari. [*awaking from amazement*] Yea, black is all, the skies,
            the stars, this world
Are black.—Mourn, Israel, your noblest died!
And how, and how, my lord, our brother drowned!
Her. My consternation holds my senses bound;
I have a tongue but scarce the use of it.—
Prince, say how that ungracious blow was dealt
To us by fate.—How did our high priest die?   [*To Pheroras.*
Pher. We laid a wager to traverse the pond
And I was beaten by his faster sweep,
But while exhausted trying to re-cross
He was provoked to show his diving strength
At seeing many sound the fish-pond's deep.
He plunging straight repeatedly did stay
A longer pause than others could endure
Beneath the water's suffocating load,
Until not re-emerging, search was made

For him who, brought to sight, was lifeless, pale
And cold. All efforts to revive him failed.
    Enter DIOPHANTUS, JOSEPH, CORINTHUS *and* SARAMELLAS.
    Her. It is a verdict passed in heaven's height
That by the flood our brother should depart.
Our heart is bleeding with the wounds of woe
We cannot utter in the shape of words.
In deepest mourning shall for thirty days
Our court and country sorrow for their priest,
Who shall with royal honors be interred.
[*They withdraw, while the curtain slowly descends. The sound
    of a muffled drum is heard.*]

ACT III.

SCENE I.

A room in the palace.

Enter ALEXANDRA, *in mourning and,* SABION.

    Alex. The news is old to me, dear friend, that they
Did long my son's destruction plan, alas,
And carry out to make me hopeless here.
And now the black assassin orders me
To wither under his abhorrent eye,
Environed by a pack of watchful spies!
My hopes, my hopes, oh Sabion, buried are
With him, save vengeance, vengeance burning in
My soul and hurling fever heat throughout
My nerves! If ever thou my child didst love,
Advise how that outrageous crime could be
Avenged.—But patience, I must wait my time.
Believe, so hot in me is vengeance that
The fiend I hate would soon my venom feel
But for good Cleopatra, who did swear
By all her means the monster to undo.
    Sab. She can through Antony his vitals wound,
And cause his downfall ere he is aware.
I know no surer means to strike thy foe,
Who hath no friend except his menial throng.
    Alex. She will not rest her head, she writes, before
That Roman calls him to account.
    Sab.   And should
His shrewdness some escape devise, what then?
    Alex. Then, Sabion, then—well, what wouldst thou begin
With all my blood-fermenting wrongs heating
Thy spirit to a vengeful pitch. What then!
I hear Aristobulus cry—Revenge!
    Sab. Here wisdom ends and accident must guide.
I should woo prudence and my hour await;
The chance may come thy thirsting hate to quench;
No mortal is invulnerable in
The lapse of time.—Or is within thy grasp
A weapon to revenge the guileful deed?

Alex. Hyrcanus could through Malchus undermine
The tyrant's might, could I to action him
Arouse; but his is not a temper to
Be moved to a resentful, hot degree,
Although I know his eyes are opening wide,
And he the foul devices of his pet
Begins to penetrate. He speaks not much
But on his furrowed brow I read his thoughts.
   Sab. Would Malchus war if him Hyrcanus prayed?
   Alex. I doubt not this, had father but the will
To ask; for hostile is Arabia to
The tyrant's rule. At all events he would
A refuge readily accord to us,
Whom black assassins menace at this court.
   Sab. How dost thou know he shares not in thy wish?
   Alex. Because I know he wishes naught but rest
And is a man who wounded would not wound;
Which notwithstanding I unceasing shall
Him with entreaties importune until
For sake of peace he to some move consents.
   Sab. Hast thou a trusty person to dispatch
With what he might be prone to send abroad?
It is not safe to place transactions of
Such import, black on white, in any hand,
Unless it rather torture's rack sustained
Than yield the purport folded in its trust.
   Alex. Describe thyself not whom since years I found
A man high-minded and with virtue fraught.
Thou hast my secrets, hast my love withal;
As on my bosom I on thine rely,
Our purpose being to effect his fall
Who mocks our faith for which we live and die.   *[Exit.*
   Sab. 'Tis good that foreheads are not made of glass
Nor thoughts of mettle to excite the eye,
Else would this world a dungeon be for knaves
To whom against my will I do belong.
The devil trains me for Abaddon's maw;
He gently seized upon my finger first,
The wrist, the arm he playingly secured;
The trunk he sneering jerked and calls it his,
And now the soul re·ists, resists in vain.   *[Exit Sabion.*

SCENE II.

At Hyrcanus' House.

Enter HYRCANUS.

Hyrcanus. What is this life? what bids this life?—A dream,
A painful, frightful dream with phantoms odd
And fleeting, fleeting, fleeting, save the woes
Which have substantial weight and withering force.
Rule, power—vanity of vanities!
The grea !—unfounded, senseless jealousy—
The great, the great, what have the great but great
Calamities, despair, heartburnings which are
To them in humbler cradles rocked unknown!
A million peasants grow old, grow white with age,

While under hundred princes ninety are
Cut off in prime of youth, or so pursued
By countless fears and traps, that hunted wolves
To them are creatures tasting bliss.—Who dreams,
In lowly cottage born. of poison, stabbing,
Of mutilation, drowning, and what not
Of treason rank-besotted courtlings hatch!—
Distrust or trust I know not whom. Upon
His head whom I did raise the guilt is put
Of that atrocity which bears me down.—
Could Herod thus repay what I for him
Have done? Thus in the bud my hope destroy,
My daughter's son, the image of his sires!
If this be so, if I conviction get
Of this, if I had proofs!—Ha, Phraates, friends,
Whose warning love I on Euphrate's banks
Unheeding gave no ear, forgive, good men,
Forgive, if I by age untaught, learn truth
Too late!—Depravity, though hideous thou
In all thy various, shifting shapes, when thee
Ingratitude begets Sheol's abysms
Rear nothing equal to thine horrid sight!—
I know the world but half and find a fool
Could wiser deal than I with him I fledged.—
Lo! there she is, all sorrow, black and tears.—[*Alexandra enters.*
My daughter brings what I am sated with,
For no addition needs my boundless grief
   Alex, My son is buried unavenged, my lord,
Should he unsorrowed rot within the dust?
How could I him forget in whom I lived!
   Hyr. The briny flood which on thy cheek descends
Will not revive him, princess, who is dead.
Two moons their faces changed since we the last
Obsequious honors him with royal pomp
Did pay, when all a people grieved with us
And with our anguish mixed their loyal tears.
But what beginning hath must have an end,
And to our mourning we should likewise set
A bound, and not proceed as if we Heaven
For gross injustice blamed.
   Alex.   Then Herod did
What Heaven bade him do. in slaying scores
Of undefended men. If such be God's
Behests then place assassins straight among
The just. and from the Decalogue efface
"Thou shalt not kill," since murder is no crime,
But meritorious is the task to slay;
Ah, and my sweet boy was murdered by God's will!
   Hyr. Interpret wiser, daughter, what I say.
Thou knowest well the meaning of my speech
As comfort given to thy bleeding heart.
Ah, what can I, an old man thus betrayed,
Do more for thee than share thy deep distress!
   Alex. I would to Heaven thou couldst my vengeance share!
   Hyr. A high priest once should I resentment breed?
   Alex. Doth not Jehovah with resentful wrath

The wicked smite who break the sacred Law?
And is not life worth having on thy part?
  Hyr. What is worth having in a time like this
When fell corruption barefaced mocks the sun
And blushing virtue must retired groan?
Behold, behold how few they are who with
The living word of the great God comply!
Yea, from their sole unto their head there is
No healthy spot but wounds and bruises
And putrifying sores, and where the voice,
The prophet to cry on their dealings—Woe!
As are the seasons in their fruitfulness
Unlike, so are the times unequal in
Their casts of men, some bringing forth a group
Of demigods, who with their spirit's breeze
Rejuvenate the unaspiring world
And make creation of her sovereign boast;
Some generating such a dwarfish kind
As would in dread before a pigmy bow
Who daring tries what sacred is profane!
This dwarfish kind is ruling in this age
So poor in men, in tyrant lords so rich!
  Alex. Alas, when man poor woman's weapon grasps,
And, impotent of action, sighs and groans,
Then to the distaff whip that craven lord
Who arrogantly claims the earth for him
And thinks his mate a creature for his whims!
Who should frail woman with her suckling babes
Defend? her flagrant wrongs who should avenge?
When did faint-heartedness itself accuse!
The times! The ages!—Granted that the tide
Of genius sweeps not unremittingly
Athwart this gloom-enwrapped world, when was
An age, a throne usurped by a slave,
A reckless murderer, whose gory hand
Defiles what by the flight of years, the blood
Of saintly martyrs consecrated is
To great Judea's heaven-guarded tribes,
With full acquiescence of the rightful head
To whom the millions for deliverance look!
Art thou an heir of Mattathias' line?
  Hyr. I hear thy mother speak in thee, proud child.
She, too, would have me fight, fight, fight!—Well, well,
Now lead the way, my mouth-prompt heroine,
And these stiff arms shall their dried sinews ply
Thy vengeance to appease!—Whom shall I stab?
Oh, there is yet force in this my trembling grip
To pierce a sleeper's undefended breast
And with assassin's fame this life depart!
  Alex. Why reason when to reason age and love
Are deaf? Now all is void and all is said
And Herod's grace will soon my sorrows end.
  Hyr. Say plainly what with dignity I could
For thee accomplish and it shall be done.
  Alex. Thou hast a friend in Malchus, why not save
Thyself and me by flying thither where
Unmenaced we may end our days in peace.

Hyr. It is thy fancy magnifying things;
There is no token of a menace here.
Alex. Wait not for thunder, fly the lightning's dart
Before the skies gr w dim, premonishment
And caution unavailing prove. The eyes
Of hundred servile courtlings rest on us;
They shadow every step, report each word
With glossy tongue, impugning mien and look,
Of credit sure by one who seeks pretense.
Hyr. Cannot Mariamne sound his dark intents
And us enlighten of his latent schemes?
Alex. Speak not of her who craves her brother's fate,
And sees a future drear as night and black.
His flippant love confessions ever flow;
To her belonged his heart, his throne, his all;
The heavens were too poor to buy her love.
So pleading, sighing, vowing he persists
Affirming he was true to her, not less
To us, to thee, myself; which is as false
As was his love to my bemourned son.
Hyr. Daughter, here swear by the tremendous God
Who with His breath can melt this massive earth,
And perjury the soul's eternal curse
Pronounced, swear that no doubt hath root in thee
About thy offspring's preconcerted death!
Alex. May Heaven never pardon my poor soul
If I in Herod's foul contrivance doubt,
Or his foreknowledge of thy grandchild's death!
Through Sabion I am certain that my heir
A terror to the tyrant's conscience seemed.
Hyr. Provide a man, I to Arabia write,
And be prepared for our impending flight.   [*Exit Hyrcanus.*
Alex. This message I in Sabion's hands shall place,
Although from Antony I hope to hear
Whom Cleopatra promised to arouse
Against the ruthless murderer of my child.
But should she fail Arabia I prefer
To this confinement in a monster's den
Where, with a rageous hatred in the soul,
I still must smile, the gall devouring which
Envenoms every atom in my blood.   [*Exit Alexandra.*

SCENE III.

A room at Herod's.

Enter HEROD and SALOME.

Herod. I should believe thee that she loves me not,
And this upon thy word who lovest not her.—
She loves me not!—Sister the jaws of hell
Are gaping at this sound!—She loves me not—
What proofs are there to make thy censure good?
Sal. Forget, dear brother, what in haste I said
Solicitous of knowing that love returned
Thou dost exuberantly nurse for her.
I may her wrong, perchance, whom by the by,
I love but less than thee, but never hate
The dearest of thy choice. She being of

Thyself a part my enmity to her
Would half be thine.
    Her.   She is a part of me;
I feel it, scent it, see it, hear it, dream
It, live on it. Mariamne is my soul
Who ebbing leaves the body lifeless, cold.—
But say, how did suspicion thy good sense
Invade? Didst thou of late her ways observe
And find her manners liable to blame?
    Sal. Since she her likeness sent to Rome——
    Her. [*interrupts*]   To Rome
Her likeness sent—by whom? I heard not this.
    Sal. Did she not tell thee that through Dellius she
To Antony her likeness sent?
    Her.   No, no!
Her lip did never utter such a word
To me. She should have told me this—she should!—
Was Dellius cause that she her likeness sent?
    Sal. Which doth excuse her having done the thing.
The Roman, struck with her excess of grace,
Did her and fair Aristobulus—then
Alive—deem beings of celestial mould
And wished their image forwarded to Rome,
To Antony who is his bosom's friend.
    Her. It throws no shade upon her honesty,
Save that she never told me aught of this.
    Sal. Perhaps, because she would no jealousy
Upstir in thy enamored breast.
    Her. [*pensively*]   That was
Not right, not as a loving wife should act.—
But thou, Salome, hadst yet more to say,
I think, when I did interrupt thy speech.—
What didst thou notice since her likeness went
To Rome?
    Sal. Did I of noting speak?
    Her.   Thou didst.—
Speak fearless, I command thee, speak! It is
Thy Herod's doom thou must confirm or free
Him from the agony of doubt.—Did aught
Mariamne which as woman thou wouldst blame?
Didst thou not say Mariamne loves me not?
    Sal. I do retract what I in love to thee
Have said unable to substantiate
What as foundation but conjecture has.
    Her. And thy conjecture might not groundless be;
Its origin and nature let me hear,
And how it took posession of thy mind.
    Sal. My king, I blush to show a weakness I
In others would reproach. I am, like thee,
Not quite unjealous of my husband's love
I which Mariamne, I suspect, is deep.
    Her. [*amazed*] Ye powers who in Hades rule—what must
I hear!—Thy Joseph and Mariamne, is
It so?—
    Sal. If apprenension leads me not astray.—
A grave offence it is to guess such things,
I know, but then he never censes of

Her wondrous loveliness to speak, and her
I smiling saw on him with queenly grace
When me she treated to a passing leer.
  Her. I am confounded! What!—Thy Joseph? Why,
I trusted him the most of all who serve   [*Enter messenger.*
Me since I rule this land.—Who is that man
Who comes?—Is Antony thy lord?—
  Mess.   His will
Enjoined me to let thy majesty
This have which I from Laodicea bring,
And ask reply.
  Her. [*takes the papers*] We will attend to thee.
                          [*Exit messenger.*
I break the seal and feel the news is grave.
My heart is throbbing faster than it should.
[*Reads*] "Impatient justice bids Judea's king
To hasten hither where a court shall try
The weight of guilt put on his royal head.
Our eagerness to justify our friend
And save his reputation now obscured
Requires Herod to be prompt in speed.
                      Antony."
I like this courtesy not much, and see
My foes are busy to promote my fall,
Above all Alexandra, who the worst
Is of the baneful crew.—I must to him
Who may as murderer arraign me and
Abridge my days, and she I worship will
Perchance my death salute and with thy fox
Divide her fair, lascivious self and bed!—
Salome, Salome, what furious tempest did
Thy hint within my inmost soul conjure!—
She loves me not!—My throne I gave could I
Her bosom's hidden longings penetrate!
But hold!—I must to Laodicea go
And will thy husband make her trusty knight
Who should her slay—such will be my command—
In case convicted of my guilt I fall.
This will them closer bring and give thee chance
To find if thy conjecture hath a ground.—
I shudder at the thought that we, perhaps,
Thy Joseph and my sweet Mariamne wrong.
  Sal Thine is but part of my profounder fear.   [*Enter Sabion.*
  Her. Be still, we shall be sure, we must be sure.—
I have a man, a subtile Greek, who will
Assist thee in the secret search.—Go send
Me Joseph here I will the task impose.—   [*Exit Salome.*
Come, Sabion, tell us what is good and new.
  Sab. [*producing a letter*] What new is this will tell, but whether
    this   ,
Be good, thy majesty may judge.
  Her. [*having read the paper*]   His head
Must off, that withered, treacherous priest!—I am
Thy debtor, Sabion.—Ha, a tyrant I!
A murderer! He would to Malchus with
His daughter fly. I was ungrateful, false!
Corinthus, ho!—The traitor dies to-day!   [*Enter Corinthus.*

Select some warriors from our valiant guard
And bring Hyrcanus well escorted here!

[Corinthus leaves, while Herod walks up and down excited.

Sab. My lord, I would not people knew I played
This game which out of loyalty to thee
I undertook. The punishment thou on
Hyrcanus wouldst inflict is, in my view,
Severe, and first consider what such step
Involves.

Her. It is considered well and weighed.

Sab. It will unfit me for thy further use
And I henceforth will be the butt of scorn.

Her. Thou must withdraw, while we the traitor question,
The rest we stifle under us—Withdraw;
Is Herod's friendship not enough for thee?

Sab. With all I can this friendship I repay.   *[Exit.*

Her. The priest is tired of his waning days
And I am tired of himself and brood,
This helps us all, him to a leap into
Hoar Abraham's lap; her to another chance
Vile Egypt to invoke; and me it rids
Of him, the last aspirant to my throne.—

Enter CORINTHUS *and* HYRCANUS *guarded.*

My holy sire, supposing thou hadst might
How wouldst a man thou treat who eats thy bread,
Professes love and gratitude to thee
Yet by his acts betrays he is thy foe?

Hyr. Treat him as foe who would as foe thee treat
For he who strives to slay thee thou mayst slay.
The Law is on his side who life defends.

Her. And did the Law's injunctions not thy arm
Unbrace when thou befouling didst my name
To Malchus on this paper send?   *[Handing a paper.*

Hyr. [glancing at the paper] I need
Not blushingly confirm what I have said.

Her. Traitor!—Not blush to say, to write what none
Alive can truthfully maintain! Not blush
To call me tyrant, murderer!—Traitor!

Hyr. There is no treason in this instrument
Unless to speak plain truth is treason in
Thy time of rule; for what I said is true,
As true as thou art more thine foe than I.

Her. Perfideous, slanderous tongue!—Away with him
And let, before an hour, me see his head!

Hyr. Ungrateful, vindictive, and reckless king!
So many guiltless heads by thee did fall,
But none so innocent and true as I
And the dear youth whose blood is on thy head.—
I am no traitor, Heaven knows it well,
But gave thee all what I by right possessed.
Nor did I envy thy exalted state
Decreed to thee by unresisting fate.
My grandchild fell by thy inhuman plan
And so I fall, no traitor but—a man.

[Hyrcanus, Corinthus, and the guards leave

Her. [*after a pause*] The last of stumbling-stones is now
   removed,
And that gray fool is wise, but wise too late.—
Still where am I? How far am I?—Oh love,
What is the substance thou art made of, craze?
A hundred thousand maidens I can have
And, like Ahasverus, the fairest choose,
Or have a dozen to beguile my time,
But vain is reason, thought, resolve! I love
Mariamne and—she loves me not.—With Joseph!—
A host of goblins whisper it at night—
With Joseph!—There he is, I must be cool.—   [*Enter Joseph.*
Thou comest in time; I think of thee.—I am
Ill-tempered, Joseph—treason—he must bleed!—
   Jos. I pity him who thus the king hath moved.
Who is the luckless fallen in thy grace?
   Her. I am too sullen, ask me not too much,
But hear wherein thou canst thy merits raise.—
I must be gone, to Antony I must;
Some state affairs of grave importance call
Me hence. Pheroras will the helm of state
Direct, while thee I guardian make of what
Is dearest in this world to me.
   Jos.   And I,
My lord, shall guard it with the dragon's eye
To whom Æetes did his fleece entrust.
   Her. Thou hast a notion what the treasure is?
   Jos. Not in the least, but be it what it may
I for its safety answer with my life.
   Her. That is a venture, man; suppose I made
Thee of a woman's virtue guard, would all
The eyes of Argus be sufficient watch?
   Jos. If there be virtue in a woman's breast
She wants no guardian to maintain it pure.
   Her. But where the woman find, thou meanst to say,
Who hath a virtue stainless in her breast?
   Jos. I mean not so, indeed; the king who claims
That thousand women furnish not one whole
Did sure no justice do the tender sex.
I nor my mother would nor wife insult
By rating lightly their devotion's worth.
   Her. How high wouldst thou Mariamne's virtue rate?
   Jos. As high, my lord, as any virtuous queen's
The story praises as devoted, pure.
Above temptation stands our beauteous queen.
   Her. No Antony or Cæsar could her win?
   Jos. I dare maintain she could a world contempt,
And more than this those potentates have not.
   Her. Thou art an idolizer of my queen.—
   Jos. If all the idols were as fair as she
Then would Jehovah's jealousy be vain.—
The queen as many votaries commands
As beauty, grace and virtue ever did.
   Her. It is a danger to be thus adored;
How easy may such consciousness entice!—
But let hair-splitting theories and phrase;
The word is pliant on the pliant lip.—

I said I must to Antony, and thee
I charge to be the queen's auspicious guard.
   Jos. |*surprised*| Define my duty and be sure 'tis done.—
I hear the charge but fail to catch the sense.
   Her. The definition hear and mark it well.—
She is a woman, mark, and wants a man
Beguiling her monotonous hours by speech
And gentle intercourse as doth befit
A queen.—She is a woman tender, sweet,
Affectionate, and wondrous soft, perchance
Solicitous about her husband's weal
Who shall be thus afar;—she wants a friend
If she must sigh to sigh with her, if she
Must weep to weep with her.—Is this not clear.—
She is a woman loving company.—
Propitious powers, I am sorely tried!
   Jos. What grim calamity impending frowns
Which clouds the humor of my lord, the king?
   Her. Ask not, I am betrayed, by friend and foe
Betrayed, my life hangs on a thread and if
I die, if never I return. my queen,
My wife—without her love I scorn the bliss
Of all the skies!—To know Mariamne in
Another's arms— Joseph, if I must die—
Now hear what I command—if I must die—
Mariamne must not live!—Why art thou pale?
Art sorry for the queen?
   Jos.   My lord, the queen!——
   Her. Yes, yes, the queen, thou wouldst my testament
Disdain should I beheaded sink, thou wouldst?—
   Jos. Let me my senses gather ere I speak.—
Are things so dark that such must be our theme?
   Her. They are so dark.—Now answer, for my time
Is short.
   Jos. I am no murderer, my lord,
Hope all will turn out brighter in the run
Of hours; would rather slay myself than rob
The world of her most precious jewel; but I
Am subject to thy royal will, and must
In all comply with thy behest.   [*Enter Pheroras.*
   Her.   Well said;
No more; I see my brother come, let us
Alone and bury deep what I have spoken.   [*Exit Joseph.*
   Pher. He wings per extra post to Eden's gates,
The naughty priest; I saw his headless frame.—
The throngs are fastly crowding every street.
The tigress' fury sparkling in their eyes;
I charged the guard to be on the alert.   [*Enter Phabatus.*
   Her. What now?
   Phab.   A bulky mob is marching toward
The palace swearing loud and clamoring
Against the king, and asking why the priest
Was slain. I never saw a rage like theirs.
   Pher. Shall I the signal give which moves the troops?
   Her. No force this time. Let me the crowd appease;
My explanation may perchance suffice.
Go tell them I will straight upon the wall

Appear and so convince them that they will
Be on my side; subdue them by discourse.
       [*To Phabatus who goes.*
And see that Sabion be among the mass.—
This hour a revolution wrought in my
Designs. This message read and judge if we
Have cause to pet the vulgar multitude.
 Pher. [*having read the paper*] A fateful document it is. Thou
  art
Accused and heavily. I read betwixt
The lines that Cleopatra moves the wheel
And he is earnest whom she holds in chains.—
Thou wilt proceed to him?
 Her.   I will!—I must!
There is no jesting with that Roman's will!—
And thou art sovereign while I am away.
Hold tight the reins of state, but curb, till I
Return, the zeal of over-hasty friends.
With moderation use, should force be found
Imperative, thy telling might. Pardon
The weak and cringing populace, but on
The leaders heavy punishment inflict.—
   Enter DIOPHANTUS; *cries of a crowd are heard.*
The crowd is wild; did not Phabatus speak?
 Dio. My lord, they listen not and cry "The king!
Let Herod speak!" And every second swells
The furious mob.—There is no time to lose.
 Her. We are not humored to apply the steel,
Instead of which this time we use the word.   [*Exeunt all.*

'

SCENE IV.

Before the gate of the court.

A crowd besieging it. PHABATUS *upon the wall.*

 Phab. I can no explanation give until
You give attention to the facts I state.
I speak the truth; or doubt you what I say?
 A Cit. Believe him not, believe him not, he speaks
Not what he thinks; he speaks not what is true,
 Another Cit. The king, the king! We want no courtling's oath;
We want to hear the king himself explain.
Why was Hyrcanus killed, a high priest slain?
 Many Voices. Why was Hyrcanus killed? The king shall say!
 A Voice. Break through the gates, down with the guard!
Break in!   [*Herod and train appear on the wall.*
 A Cit. Now there is Herod; silence, hear him! He looks
On us and smiles. He waves his hand; be still!
 Her. My fellow-countrymen and loyal friends.—
 A Cit. He says we are his fellow-countrymen
And loyal friends.
 A Voice.   Keep still, thou babbling jack!
 Her. My fellow-countrymen and loyal friends,
To show the rate at which I set your love
I stand here ready to defend myself
Against the fools who say that Herod did
Hyrcanus slay. I slew him not, he slew

Himself by forcing me to strive in self-
Defense, which is, according to our Law,
No crime, but sacred duty on our part.
Where is a man who loving wife and child
And being threatened by a treacherous foe
Would unconcerned thus his life expose
And not retort the meditated stroke?
Is there one here who would his foe not wreck?
I hear no voice, that is I hear no lie.
No man would lose his life without defense.
And now decide, suppose you had a friend
Possessing all the love your hearts can give,
Dividing all your wealth and plans with you,
And you discovered him in league with one
Who is the deadliest of your bitter foes,
Would you not reckon him a traitorous heart?
Who says he would not, says a shameful lie.—
Such is the nature of my case. You think
Hyrcanus was an old, good man; I thought
Like you until this fatal paper—which
You all may read—convinced me he was not;
For Malchus of Arabia is my foe
With whom this paper proves him leagued against
Myself and land—hear you—against your land!
Against this country did Hyrcanus plot,
His hand outlined the scheme here black on white.
If to destroy a traitor be a crime
Then prove it to a court I shall appoint.
                          [*Exeunt Herod and train.*
    A Cit. Who would believe it of the holy man,
And yet the king doth say he can it prove.   [*Enter Sabion.*
    Another Cit. He says he had it written black on white.—
Thou, Sabion, tell us whether all be true.
    Sab. I knew beforehand you would ask me this,
But spare the answer me which is too sad.
A friend of mine he was—Heaven pardon him!
    A Voice. Then go we hence, the king has told the truth!
    A Cit. [*shaking his head*] I have my thoughts and others have
        them too.
To say and unsay, he said, I said, we
Said, well, Hyrcanus something had to say
As well, but he is mute and slain untried,
This pinches me.—To slay a man untried!
Why, blockheads are they who believe his guilt.
            [*He leaves muttering some words; the others follow him.*

Herod's bedchamber.

MARIAMNE *on a divan, he kneeling before her.*

Herod. No, waste these pearls not, goddess, rolling from
Thy star-outsparkling eyes! This precious flood
The gods make jealous of Hyrcanus' death
Who lives in thee a thousand thousand lives!
He is not dead for whom a seraph weeps.

Mari. He is, alas! and sees the sun no more!
The dear benignant, hoary, sacred head
To whom the savage Parthian bowed in awe
Thus fallen is forever, buried, dead;
By thee, whom he did raise, did love, did back
In what thy interest required, slain,
Beheaded like a culprit guilty of
Unheard-of crimes!—Hyrcanus, no! there is
No spot on thy illustrious honored name!
He traitor!—King, thou couldst as well the sun
Of giving birth to night accuse because
Of shades through his departure dominant.
He called thee tyrant, murderer, which to
Disprove thou both these qualities on him
Didst grossly test!—Who would a court not fly
Where all the vices find a genial home?
Treason to save one's life! No, treason in
Thy judgment, is to be an Asmonean!
    Her. [*rising*] Celestial shrew, yea, right in one respect
Is thy unfounded, strange accuse. In thee,
Proud Asmonean, it looks like treason thus
To hold my angled heart and spurn my love.—
Aye, torture, sting degenerate manhood in
Thy too devoted, too uxorious fool!
Mariamne not but Herod of us two
The woman's garb should wear, and thou, untamed,
Inexorable as thou art, unmoved,
A coat of mail shouldst thy habiliment make.
Till now, sweet madam, what of Herod thou
Hast seen was not that Herod dreaded by
The desert's warlike hordes. I can a shape,
A face, a frown, an eye so horrible
Assume that Satan in his fiendish ire
Less dreadful is to mortal gaze than I!—
But Heaven, this fairy makes a fawn of me,
And every effort to regain my self
Proves more and more I am a fettered slave!
Did Lilith not to thee her charm impart
That chains the youth and wringing rives his heart?
That makes him sigh and burn with loving rage
Who vainly seeks nepenthe his wounds to assuage!
    Mari. I used no potions to unman thy nerves
Nor any charm to capture thus thy heart.
    Her. No magic draughts, the witchcraft lies in thee,
Enchantress, whose resistless eye a fire
Drives through the veins so violent and hot
That Lethe's wave, adjoining it, would boil.—
Mariamne, by all those powers who the skies
Control, by the eradiations of
The lucent orbs, I swear I am unmanned,
Undone, if I to Antony proceed
With doubt oppressing me about thy love!
Say frankly, woman, if I ought to strive
For love's delights I yet may taste alive;
If not, my queen, I will resign my breath
And seek my peace in rayless, hopeless death!

Mar. [*rising*] Our infants wear thy image, king; I see
They love their father whom I should not hate;
Till I am down with whelming misery
I am resolved to face my cruel fate!
The dear are gone who made my life so sweet,
My last of sires with Hyrcanus died;
They are in Heaven where the pious meet
Who vile temptation here beneath defied.
Oh, could I hope the high priests to embrace
In yonder heights where youth doth never fade,
To see my brother with his beaming face
In garb angelic with the saints parade,
I should be tempted this my heart now broke
With overpowering woes, soul-wringing sighs
To open by a steel's well-pointed stroke
And with my angels weep in blissful skies.—
But I am bound my earthly course to run,
The mortal's sorrows feel until my end;
For He who kindled the enkindling sun
Forbids frail man to fall by his own hand.
I live and bear resigned my heavy lot,—
Go, king, depart, Mariamne hates thee not.
Her. [*embracing her*] So much is little yet it bids me live!
                 [*The curtain decends, while he holds her embraced.*

ACT IV.

SCENE I.

A room at Salome's

Enter EURYCLES.

Eurycles. A jest is worth a jest and for the sport
I in Salome's bed enjoy I can
Afford to draw in her behalf on my
Unquestioned honesty, and, having made
Of Herod's sister a debauching drab
Indeed, I should, this drab to please, by some
Contrivance blast the reputation of
His virtuous queen. Why Joseph loathe and me
Adore here Satyr had his fun, if fun
In woman's inconsistency there be.
I am as sure of Joseph's innocence,
As sure that fair Mariamne has no thought
Of guilt, as I of my adultry have
No doubt. But then the king commanded her
To serve, and she hath taught me how, and I
Have told her, ay, and cuckolded her fop
Who dreams not that he gets his portion from
My saintship second-hand.—Till midnight I
Till morn the dupe; such is our program since
The king is off.—Lo! there the horned sage.- -   [*Enter Joseph.*
My best, sincere good morrow, honored sir.

Jos. Good morrow, wakeful friend. Please tell my wife,
Whom I have left asleep, that I must on
The queen wait ere the king arrives. She knows
Not yet that Herod comes to-day against
The rumor whispered of his fall. He comes
Sustained in all his dealings here, and my
Surprise I with the queen divide.
 Eury.   She will
Delighted be such tidings to receive.
She is mock-widow now two months or so.
 Jos. She will, she will, I have no doubt she will!
Six weeks are past since he hath left the queen
And this is long for hearts to be apart.
 Eury. My wife and self could stand it thrice that time.
But we are Greeks, the Hebrews being strict
And thinking guilt what Spartans deem but sport.
No Moses could for Hellenes legislate.
Lycurgus' code permits no property
To be the one's and not the other's good,
And woman's beauty he did part make of
The common wealth. My wife is thine and thine
Is mine, such is the Spartan's liberal view.
 Jos. In vast Judea none the Grecian ways
Admires more than Herod, but in this,
I know too well he is not half a Greek.
The king is jealous of his eunuchs' eyes
That they, like his, Mariamne's graces view,
And woe to him on whom suspicion fell
Of being favored by the beauteous queen!
This to no angel Herod would forgive.
 Eury. I rather, then, with Cerberus the gate
Of hell would guard than watch this monarch's wife.
The envious gods, when Love forsook the skies
To sweeten here the mortal's ruthful lot,
To turn her bliss into a plague to man,
Of all the fevers made a phantom black
Which haunts and maddens him who loves too much;
This fearful spectre Jealousy they called.
 Jos. He made me warden not with my consent,
But he shall find her true and be content
If what for him she feels he may call love.—
I am a parrot, zounds. The queen might to
The groves before I come. The sun is high.
Farewell!—Forget not what I asked.—Adieu.   [*Exit.*
 Eury. I see not why I should this person wreck
Who treats me hospitably in this house,
Not like a servant which I feign to be,
But like a man his equal every inch
And what have I against the sweetest queen
That hates the plotter who her kinsman slew,
And shuns my harlot, whom I neither love?
But if I moralize why am I here
Where honest men are out of vision puffed?—
I see her near, and must prepare for love.   [*Enter Salome.*
I should be gallant till I see my way.—
Good morrow, princess,—what, so early up?

Sal. Ah, false adorer! early thus for thee?
Eury. Thou must not misconstrue my anxious love;
For hours I hang about that entrance there
As erring pilgrim gazing at the East
To see the sun illumine his dark path;
Yet for thy dreamy slumber I my rest
Would give; for, though I suffer, half the pain
Is taken when I know thy dreams are sweet.
Oh could but ever I repose with thee!
   Sal. Thou knowest well my soul's most ardent wish
Is in thy arms to dream, but not until
The ground is clear can we have rest. The hour
Is pressing and our future on thy nerve
Depends. My Greek intrepidly must act,—
Now hear the scheme I during night devised:
My husband, whom I hate as thee I love,
A secret order from the king received
To slay the queen should he be slain abroad.
By fine suasion I did prompt him, ere
The king returns, the order to divulge
To her, whose fiery temper will revolt
Against a love so cruel in its craze,
Her prudence give to indignation way;
And bitter hatred she will vent on him
Whom new success will stimulate to pride,
And disappointment drive to wild extremes.
This moment seizing we must deal the blow,
Affirming straight that criminal intercourse
My cuckold and the queen together leagued,
His gross betrayal backing our accuse.
This daring measure will our foes remove.
   Eury. Will words suffice to test such heinous guilt?
   Sal Ay, for the moment they will surely work.
The king's decision will be quick and sharp,
And what is done he never can undo
   Eury. Their death alone could make success secure.
   Sal Their death alone can calm my brother's wrath
Who in his rage did never try to think.—
I count upon the temper of a king.
   Eury, And I my life on thy experience set
And thy directions shall my compass be.
Command when it is time to act, I stand
A slave to thy unhindered will, knowing
Thou wilt for much not sacrifice my heart.
   Sal. [*takes his hand*] One moment yet let us in soft delight
In half-dusk taste the pleasures of sweet love.
Come, dearest Greek, have thou my consort's right;
That chamber be my nest and I thine dove.   [*Exeunt both.*

SCENE II.

A room at the queen's.

Enter ALEXANDRA *and* MARIAMNE.

Alex. I say, the time is come for us to fly;
Pheroras will the throne ascend, and he
Will sweep us from this earthly round, The grave
Or Egypt—choose the best of these.

Mari. My babes,
My pretty babes, what will become of them!

Alex. Become of them! They will be men and may
Be kings once distant from this land of woe.
Had with my son I fled this cursed seat,
I would not helpless thus and desolate
My child bewail. But Heaven dull'd my sense
That time; and now I pray thee let us fly!

Mari. We trust a rumor which our foes perchance
Have spread to see how Herod's death would us
Affect and thus our disaffection test.
If Herod fall, Mariamne would not weep;
I never loved the man whom now I loathe
With all the madness of a tortured heart.
But he may live and frustrate our attempt.
We should await what Joseph has to say.

Alex. We should our lives not place in Joseph's hand
Whose outward shows I would not much confide.

Mari. He is a man in whom I faith repose,
Although I hate the female he calls wife.   [*Enter Joseph.*
He comes! Why spoke we not of cheerful days?—
Thou art our theme, good Joseph. and some news
Of moment we expect to hear. What is
The rumor worth about the king's return?

Jos. Who told the queen that Herod is returning?

Mari. Is he returning? And that whisper hath
Nor hand nor foot? Speak, Joseph, and my doubts
Dispel.

Jos. I think that minutes will thy doubts
Disperse, for if the tidings be correct
The king in minutes will the queen embrace.

Mari. Then Herod lives and all are stories forged?

Alex. And Antony confirmed him in rule?

Jos. My knowledge goes not further than, he comes;
The rest, my queen and princess, he will tell.

Alex. A great surprise, for sure, a great surprise.—

Mari. The idle tongues should be cut off who thus
Invent good people to confound. A change
Like this not every mind can bear. I scarce
Can realize that all was not a dream.

Jos. Which shall make room for sweet reality.
The loving consort dearer is to thee,
Fair queen, than to the rest the glorious king,
And so much greater thy rejoicing is
Than ours, although I would the last not be
Nor least to welcome such a gracious lord.

Mari. If he the quality of consort would
By royal deeds display as he the rate
Of friendship doth by high rewards attest,
I would be queen in other sense than name.

Jos. My most admired, worshipp'd, virtuous queen,
I here in presence of her princely grace,
Thy fair and noble mother, must maintain—
Thou dost the king, my lord's affection wrong.
There lives no man beneath this country's sky,
No man as far as Rome's vast empire doth
Extend, who so adores and loves his wife

As Herod doth his beauteous queen. Ay, what!
His quality of husband not display?
He is a lover still, the husband's calm
Being enkindled by the lover's rage.
There is a mania in our monarch's love
Which is intenser than his fear of death.
None better knows it than myself. I have
Such strong and irrefutable proofs that he
The queen more than his life does love that I
Must wonder at thy unaccountable doubts.
I knew what love is when I Herod knew.
    Alex. Why not, good Joseph, undeceive the queen
Who failed hitherto to sound his love
Which, loud in words, was beggarly in deed?
    Mari. Thou art my friend, my husband's confidant;
If aught thou knowest would the difficulties
Remove betwixt the king and me, then speak,
Since reticence, though prudent otherwise,
In such a case resembles much a wrong.
    Jos. A base Delilah did a Samson wreck,
What weighs a Joseph in Mariamne's hand?
    Mari. [*smilingly*] I hit it now! A secret is it not?
A secret in thy breast should me convince,
That I am terribly beloved, adored!
Fy! Joseph, with those second hand confessions!
Man, mock a wretched woman not! To such
A vulgar love I noble hate prefer.
    Jos. My queen!—
    Mari.   Fy, fy! To whisper secrets on
A wife, a queen, and keep her ignorant
About herself—if that be love, Joseph,
Then neither thou dost love know, friend, nor he.
    Jos No, madam, that is love, divinest love
Which Herod bears his queen; and here the proof.—
Though this divulgement blast me I will speak
To vindicate my lord the loving king!—
Know that before the king took leave of you
And Laodicea made his journey's goal,
He did to me his inmost grief impart.
In broken accents he did groaning speak,
And, sighing, swore that, should misfortune him
Betide, he scorned death, but would amid
The saints of Paradise Mariamne miss;
I should him promise—well, a whim, a freak—
I should him promise not to let him wait
In heavens long for thee, but——
    Mari. [*impatient*]   Finish, man!
But cut my throat or stab, no?——
    Jos.   Never spoke
He such a phrase as this, and sure he meant
It better than it sounds.—In Paradise
Without thy company there was no bliss,
He thought. It is a whim, but still his love!—
    Mari. For monsters like that beast in human frame
There is a pit in hell! Sweet Eden would
Turn black at his abominable sight!
Oh Joseph, silence! speak not of the fiend

Whose love I dread! Oh filthy soul, oh snake
In manly shape!—I thank thee for this love
On which my bitter hatred feeds.
   Jos.   If thou
The use of strong reproach wilt not forbear
And base it on my frank discourse I have
My ruin conjured; for treason would to him
Appear what I well-meaning to defend
Him have exposed.   [*Trumpets are heard without.*
   Alex.   They sound the king's approach
And I no mission have him to receive.   [*Exit Alexandra.*
   Mari. Nor I, distempered as I am and wroth.—
Excuse me, Joseph, I am sick at heart —
I cannot smile now that my sense is galled,
And in my heart the blood fermenting boils.
Be not dejected, friend, Mariamne knows
The goblin who that fien·ish order gave.   [*Trumpets are heard.*
'Tis he saluted by the guards. Oh God,
Now fortify my soul to front the beast
When he arrives at his accursed lair
To glut his bestial lust on me! Ah, sires,
Immortal figures, who with Israel's staff
The dear inalienable sacred rights of man
Imprinted on the brow of time, from your
Supernal seat of bliss the Power benign
Invoke to teach me how to end my state
Of untold wretchedness!   [*Exit Mariamne.*
   Jos.   Fool, fool, fool! Would
I had a score of cries to proclaim
I am a long-eared, braying, stupid ass!
To sap thus studiously my own support
In such a coxcomb way and have a brain!
My wife's suggestion following I fall.   [*Trumpets are heard.*
I could bite off my tongue so do I hate
The looseness of that boneless, babbling piece!

Enter HEROD, PHERORAS, PHABATUS, DIOPHANTUS, SABION, COR-
   INTHUS, SARAMELLAS, *and a train of armed guards.*

   Her. [*surrounded by his court.*] My prince, grandees, my lords
     and loyal friends,
Returning with due honors from the man
Whom continents obey, and having all
Our foes by friendliness or force subdued,
We now may turn an eye to peaceful arts,
To works of beauty and of noble taste.
In fair proportions with embellishments
Of rarest kind our Sanctuary nears
The crowning touch, and round it soon a vast,
Impregnable citadel encompassing
Shall rise, enclosing habitations large
And solid, wearing Roman ensigns on
The front and Antony's immortal name,
To whom we purpose other monuments
To set in token of our love to him.
To honor Cæsar we Olympian games
From Grecian soil import, and for this end
Erect a vast, commodious edifice

With all belongings of a racing space.
Our plan is made to see new cities rise,
And various structures shall this land adorn
In memory of those to us endeared.
All this will stimulate our people's mind, *
And those in league with us may see how we
Fidelity and friendship on the brow
Of rocks engrave.   My land I find in peace,
For which I thank you, prince, grandees, my lords.—
                    [*Exeunt all save Herod and Joseph.*
I miss Mariamne's welcome, Joseph.—How
Conceive the absence of the queen? She was
In time of my return apprised?
    Jos.   She was
My lord, and waited in this hall until
A while before thy coming was a third
Time by the trumpet signaled, when of some
Unpleasant feeling overcome, she left,
Assuring me she ought to be excused;
She was not well, not in the frame of mind
To cheerfully receive my lord, the king.
    Her. What may account for such a sudden change?
    Jos. The queen was in her humor ruffled when
This morn I came with news of thy return.
The princess, Alexandra, was with her
And went the moment I the news conveyed.
    Her. They were consulting and by thee disturbed?
    Jos. Methought they were, my lord, but what, my skill
Could draw no inference. I caught no word,
No syllable to serve me as a key
To what their consultation might have been.
    Her. There is a knot which I shall cut at once!   [*Exit Herod.*
    Jos. The cut may reach my throat. I am undone!
I dug my grave encouraged by mine wife;
I must to her; although the gates of hope
Are closing over me, she may yet see
A way.—The tongue, the tongue! oh snaky thing!   [*Exit.*

SCENE III.

The Queen's bedchamber.

Mari. [*her hands folded*] Ye sacred ministers of love and grace
Who from Sheol's profoundest deep the ghosts
Of purged sinners to immortal heights
Uplift, show me the path to hope from this
Unblessed, fearful, bloody labyrinth
Wherein my bleeding soul entangled strives!
That hellish agent who my dearest slew
And me delivered to a courtier's knife,
That murderous fiend my husband call and lord,
Receive him in the arms of love, my bed,
Myself divide with him and smile—and smile!
Ha, basilisk, how do thy likeness in
My innocents' complexion I abhor!
Oh patience, softness feminine, the tongue,
The tear, the tear, the tongue is all we have
Our blackest outrages on demons to

Avenge! -My grandsire slain, my brother slain,
Myself for slaughter marked, abused, and I
That hell-hound's grisly volume on my hips
Support!—No, sacred ancestry, I feel
Your unpolluted, martial blood in me
Revolt against submission to a fate
So dire!—Herod, I am prepared to meet
Thee now; walk in, I am not what I was!—   [Enter Herod.
    Her. I hear my name, but not a loving sound.
Thy wild excitement, queen, betokens evil.
My heart is still the same, but thine is not,
And thy reception tells me love is past.—
    Mari. And all the blessings of thy house are past;
Nay, never blessings did on it alight,
For curse and blessing never did unite.
    Her. [*trying to suppress his rage*] Imperious, proud, uncon-
        querable queen,
How long shall I a beggar worship thee
Who thus repels me like the vilest slave?
In awe before me twenty millions bow,
Great Antony embraces me as friend,
At my command the desert turns a town,
And with my warlike arm I won a state—
Shall I forever live in fear of such
A peevish, uninstructed scold?—Woman,
If I guess right, the message of my death
Would be more welcome than my presence here.
Deny it woman, or believe I shall
Ungently touch thy haughty, huge conceit!
Deny it, or by this my sword which, from
The clutches of thy kindred wrung this throne,
I shall a dreadful vengeance take on thee!
For if I were one-eyed and thou the eye,
I, to allay my all-devouring rage,
Would pluck thee from my socket's cave and cast
Thee to the dogs!
    Mari. [*pale with wrath*] Now listen, I will speak
And mirror in my speech thy horrid self!
Thou mayst the rabble with thy threats appall,
Or frighten Bedouins with thy gory fame,
But I am callous to thy savage frowns;
Can well resist thy foul, unbridled tongue,
And bare my breast before thy dagger's point!
Aye, speak to all the world, inhuman king,
But not to me of thy heroic feats.
I know thy story written with the blood
Of noblest hearts thy greed untimely pierced!
Thou owest Rome, but not thy sword, this crown
And hast no friend beyond thy sordid stock!
Uncounted widows, when their orphans weep,
Cry Herod! Herod! in their infants' ear,
And curse the hour of thy unholy birth!
Thy menial slaves my princely brother drowned;
By thine behest they carried out the crime;
My grandsire raised thee with a parent's love;
By him persuaded I became thy bride;
By him prepared thou art Judea's king,

And yet, thy craven fears to calm, his blood,
A high priest's sacred blood did flow!—But as
If tortured with a blood-hound's thirst for gore,
Or with that monster's unconceivable greed
Who on his young his beastly hunger gluts,
Thy wolfish instinct on destruction bent
Now eyes in me an undefended prey!—
I should not thee survive, unspeakable fiend;
Deny it, monster, or my loathing bear!
 Her. [*in a paroxysm of rage*] Ha, traitor, traitress!—Night and
  blackness, ha!
The hell is yawning!—Go, thou art a whore. [*Strikes her.*
With Joseph, yea with Joseph!—Vengeance, death! [*Exit.*
 Mari. Now he the poison bears.—He struck me, well,
That hand will rot, while he is yet alive.—
He can my bosom pierce, but not my name
Befoul.—With Joseph!—Fiend, thy thoughts are like
Thyself, demoniac, foul and black.—A stone
Is off my breast; I told him all, he foams
Like raging tiger with the deathful shaft
In him.—Vengeance, death.—I mock them all;
I with my babies pray, and praying fall. [*Exit Mariamne.*

SCENE IV.

A room at Joseph's.

Enter JOSEPH *and* SALOME.

 Sal. My fault it is that thou hast little sense
And the last second didst select to say
What weeks ago thou prudently couldst do
And give her time to rumiuate the truth.
Of course, I should as well be mad to learn
The measure, knowing not the gentler cause.
 Jos. I found no means to pacify her mind
Imbued with deep distrust against the king.
She never ought to learn the purposed act
Which any woman's gentleness would ruffle;
For who can justly say that he was right?
 Sal Ah, Joseph sides with her, it is too clear.
 Jos. I side with her and any one in right.
Thou art her enemy, she taunting oft
Thy lowly birth, and shunning intercourse
With thee on equal terms.—That is not right,
But justifies not wrong by her endured.
 Sal. She is my bitter foe and thou art sure
Her friend, that is thou art my bitter foe.
She hates thy wife and thou dost take her part
Who will, should her conteutious haughtiuess
A quarrel seek, not spare thy name nor life.—
What is it driving thee in such a haste? [*To Eurycles who enters.*
 Eury. Madam, dear sir, the king is raging, froth
Upon his lips. He runs from room to room,
Swears, cries: "Coriuthus!—The guard—traitor—death—
Veugeance—with Joseph—traitress,"—and so forth.—
His mood affrights me, madam; madness stares
In his revengeful eye.—I dread his rage.

Jos. I must be gone; the lightning darts on me.—
He said, "With Joseph?" was it so?
Eury.   Quite so.
" With Joseph—traitress," I distinctly heard.
Jos. I dare, in his delirium, not confront
The king.—I apprehend he knows it all.—
I must withdraw until his wrath subsides.   [*Exit.*
Sal. Unmanly coward, thus to run away!—
Our fortune smiles; now be a man.—She is
Adultress, hearest thou?—This will seal their fate. [*Enter Herod.*
There is the king, Medusa in his look.—
Her. Ha, monkey, vile baboon, licentious ape!
To hell with him!—Where is thy bed's companion,
Thy Joseph, wench, where is thy man?—
Sal.   Protect
Me Heaven!—Thou art as white as death!—He is
Away.—
Her. Away!
Sal He ran away.—
Her.   He ran
Away! This earth no cavern hath to hide
The lecherous ape I hunt.—Salome, ha!
Thy husband—treason—with my wife, the queen;
His fear to face me doth confirm his guilt!
Sal. I warned thee in time;—no news for me.
Her. Eternal agony!—No news for thee?
Sal. Ay, brother, let that man there speak.—
Her.   That man!
Sal. That man, thy faithful servant, Eurycles,
Hath brought to light what my suspicion wove.
Her. Hath brought to light! All doubt is gone!—To light!—
Speak fellow!—Ah, it is the Greek I gave
Thee.—Speak, my dreadful witness!—No, speak not!—
The guard, Corinthus!—Bring the traitor here!—
They do not come!—
Sal.   They hear thee not.—Oh dear,
Support it like a man and cast that wife
Away!
Her. And cast that wife away! Am I
Awake, asleep? Is this a vision I
Am passing through?—This is myself, and this
Salome, and there the Greek, the witness.—Ha!
Speak witness, give me certainty I hear!—
If I am dreaming, then I dream in hell!
Eury. My dreadful lord, would Cheop's pyramid
Had been on me before I witnessed what
I now must test.—I think it was not all
His crime; the guilty intimacy was
By tempting hints and demonstrations on
The queen's part brought about.
Her.   Keep cool, keep cool,
Poor Herod, cool.—Thou sayst the queen has done
The whole by hints and demonstrations, what
Of her advances didst thou note of late?
If more be known to thee let all me know.
Eury. Some time ago the princess with a charge,
A private errand, sent me to her lord

Attending on the queen. As I on toes
The known apartments did approach, my ears
Absorbed the sound of kissing lips and speech
So soft and amorous that envy struck
My heart, and I was tempted to surprise'
The happy turtle sport, myself unseen.
Amazement seized me when, on drawing nigh,
I through a half-shut door beheld the queen
And treasurer in sweet delight embraced,
Against a divan leaning, she burying
Her head beneath his beard. "And is it true,"
She said uprearing gracefully her head,
"That he consign'd me to a murderous death?"
Whereto the lover did affirming nod.
I then the queen heard clearly say: "He must
Not live, the vile plebeian whom my soul
Abhors!"—
 Her. Enough, these are her words; enough,
I have no wife, had never one!—Corinthus!
Phabatus!—Why, are they asleep?—Oh, they all
Have wives and friends, I am the only wretch,
A solitary wretch enthroned and crowned.—
Go, summon the unsympathetic slaves! [*To Eurycles who goes.*
I'll have thy traitor piecemealed inch by inch.
First he, my harlot after him.—She falls,
Though with her sink the skies.—I must see blood! [*Exit Herod.*
 Sal. The loosened rock doth from the cliff descend
With unresisting, all-uprooting force,
I see my foes beneath its fragments bend
And buried in the wreckage of its course!   [*Exit Salome.*

SCENE V.

School-room in the Temple. A crowd of scholars lowly seated
around Matthias.

 1st Scholar. I pondered long on what the Scriptures say:
"And thou shalt love the Lord thy God with all
Thy heart, with all thy soul, with all thy might."
But know not, master, to define the verse.
Are these three faculties not one in three?
 Matt. Not quite, my son.—They all are Heaven's gifts
On man bestowed; though interwoven they
Are three in function and in end diverse.
In one the feeling's heavenly germ is laid;
The other is the throne of reason's rule;
The third in action shows supreme command.
Thy heart's suggestions follow when ou mild
And charitable deeds it bends thy sense,
But leave no room within for instincts low
Which desecrate that holiest of seats.
As to thy soul, it heavenward aspires,
The star-paved quarry whence that gem is cut;
Unless encumbered with the lead of sin
She will, like fire, seek ethereal space
And never feel the thirst for wisdom quench'd
Until invested with immortal sight
To view all wonders, freed of earthly clay.

In might man's greatness and his danger lies.
By it he holds dominion o'er this world,
A sceptred monarch of all nature's realm;
By it abused he is this nature's curse.
And woe to man when might is centred in
A tyrant's unrestricted hand! for naught
Is holy to a power founded on
The wrecks of human liberty divine!
  2d Schol. Allows the Law no vengeance on such foes?
  Matt. With all thy might is written in the Law,
Which signifies, defend thy Sanctuary
At cost of life. These restless, fleeting days,
When sacrificed in struggling for our God,
Procures a sweet eternity of bliss.
  3d Schol. Why fight we not against tyrannic rule?
Why purge we not this place of heathen games?
  4th Schol. The Roman eagle on the Temple's door
By Herod planted, is it not a shape,
An image branded in the Decalogue?
  5th Schol. The giant statues reared to pagan chiefs
Within the precincts of Jerusalem,
From Dan to far Beer-Sheba, heat the blood
Of myriads ready to wipe out the fell
Abomination from our sacred midst!   [*Enter Judas Saripheus.*
  Matt. The hour is not auspicious now, methinks,
To rouse rebellion in this chastised land;
But when it comes I shall my pupils lead
To martyr death or brilliant victory.
  Judas Saripheus. I find commotion even in these rooms,
Sequestered though they are from public stir.
But all creation should with uproar shake,
And cleanse of prodigies her sacred face!
  Matt. [*while the scholars rise*] What is the latest of untoward
      events?
  J. Sari. The most preposterous of all yet known.—
The queen is prisoner by the king's command.—
  Matt. The queen, Mariamne?—
  J. Sarip.   Mariamne is condemned
To die the death of infamy and shame;
And Joseph died a partner of her guilt.—
  Matt. Joseph, the king's most favorite confidant?
  J. Sarip. Salome's lord and Herod's treasurer
Beheaded fell accused of criminal lust.
  Matt. By whom accused, and testified by whom?
  J. Sarip. By Herod, Herod, Herod; these are three
Who in their methods never disagree.
  Matt. Would God divested him of rule and sense!
  J. Sarip. The half of thy petition granted is
Already; for gossip says his wits are gone.
  Matt. [*to his scholars*] Good boys, it might be time for us to act,
But move no finger till we meet again.
We shall meantime our thoughts mature, our means
Employ, and, shunning rashness, carry out
Our plan   Of Judas Maccabæus read;
His life will ripen you for glorious deed!
                [*The scholars disperse all excited.*

J. Sarip. Why should we wait when urgency invites?
Impatient for a leader call the tribes
And every eye is turned on thyself.
Thou art the high priest whose appeal will fire
The masses to determined dauntlessness.
Let us resist the monstrous tyranny
Which strives to paganize our holy land!
   Matt. I feel not warlike, brother, at this hour,
A softer sentiment possessing now
My tender properties.—The queen, I fear,
Dies innocent, a guiltless victim of
An infamous scheme. While as a minister
Of the Most High for sacred freedom I
Am bound to war, the gentler duty of
Consoling innocence in dark distress
Due preference claims, and I must see the queen.
   J. Sarip. Well thought; compassion first and then revenge.
   Matt. Yea, I must see her, must console her; come,
Her dreadful husband will this boon her grant.
   J. Sarip. And I will to her mother go not less
Deserving of compassion's soothing speech,
She, though not stainless in her dealings here,
Hath borne a life's long sorrowful career.   *[Exeunt both.*

SCENE VI.

ALEXANDRA *and* Æsop *in one of her rooms.*

   Alex. My daughter, too, and I must childless sink
With unextinguish'd vengeance in my blood!
My daughter, too, thus shame-polluted falls,
And Joseph slain, who cannot clear her name!
Still this despair and now the worst I stood;
The skies are cruel, Æsop, yea they are!
   Æsop. The times are rotten but the skies are just,
And I am wicked or I would not breathe
To such a crumbling age to see my hopes
All buried, ere I broken die! I bore
Them in these arms, the drowned high priest and
The gracious queen. Untamed, ferocious beast
Would cringe in playful mood around the babes,
And savage Parthians melted at their sight,
So sweet bloom'd gentle infancy in them.
But envious fortune is a jealous slut
Who gives us most that we may lose the most!
Now all my prayers centre but in one—
I wish to go now that my joys are gone.
   Alex. I hate this life and love this earth no more,
Yet would I live to see that tyrant's gore
Who will my daughter slay, who slew my heir,
Who slew my father, driving to despair
A gnashing woman who finds not a tear
To weep her woes upon this doleful sphere.
                          [Enter Judas Saripheus.
Come, holy man, and let a mourner see
What faith can do against calamity.   *[Exit Æsop.*
   J. Sarip. Madam, If Job's afflictions would thy self
Betide, redoubled joys the Lord of Hosts

Bestows on such as question not his ways
And in the mortal's weak discernment doubt.
   Alex. My source of joy is drying in the ground
And shame is added to my boundless woes.
The cursed hand that holds Judea chained
And Zion makes the seat of heathen gods,
It struck my son in prime of budding youth,
Polluting now my daughter's virtuous name
Without a knight her innocence to plead!
What owe these tribes not to my ancestors
Whose guiltless progeny defenseless falls
Exterminated by a tyrant's hand;
Alas, no steel, no voice resounding in
Their dear defense!   When was a being slain
Without protest!
   J. Sarip.   Protest! dear princess, all
Our tribes protest against the yoke they bear
Which naught but action can revolting break.
   Alex. The actors tarry and the yoke is hard.
No, no!   The heroes of Judea lived;
This craven age will vegetating sink
Who have the tongue but not the nerve to deal
With manly courage, death-provoking front.
Hath Herod hosts Antiochus had not,
Whose armed legions not their manhood chilled
Who strove resolved for sacred rights to bleed?
   J. Sarip. We are not mettled like those matchless men
Whose glorious feats our people's story grace,
Yet do we know what can be done or not.—
It is not Herod, princess, whom we fear,
But him to combat means to combat Rome
And those dread armies of resistless dash
To whom the world reluctantly submits.
What wouldst thou have, suppose we followed thee?
   Alex. I would the tyrant's power overthrow,
By stabbing him who broke so many hearts.
   J. Sari. And let Pheroras or a heathen rule?
   Alex. A heathen rather than a half-breed Jew
Who is no heathen, but a heathen's slave!
What could be worse than Herod wielding power!
Nay, any change would for the better tend,
Since none so low but would some feeling have,
Some awe for age, some reverence for the wise,
Some love for truth, regard for royal blood,
For guiltless life so monstrously destroyed.
   J. Sarip. A change is nigh if Heaven speeds our work.
We are not idle in our holy cause,
But would not rashly act without design,
Without a prospect of a fair success.
A valiant band in readiness awaits
The signal of the leaders they revere
To strike the blow with overwhelming force,
And spread revolt throughout this scourged land.
The queen's arrest unsettled our resolve,
For in our sadness drowned is all revenge.
   Alex. Vain is your sympathy, my daughter falls,
Unless her rescue you in time effect

Before that orb athwart the azure rolls,
Or she will rise to the divine Elect.
I have no hope, my heart tells me she dies,
But meet we will and weep in yonder skies.

       [*She leaves followed by Judas Saripheus.*

A C T　V .

SCENE I.

A room in the palace.

Enter HEROD *and* PHERORAS.

Herod. What said the traitor? He denied his lust?
Oh, had the demon but a score of necks
I should at leisure crack them one by one!　　___|
  Pher. He said he died unguilty of the crime.
His wife did lie; the queen was innocent
And thou was maddened by mean jealousy.
Thou wouldst thy madness rue, but rue too late.
  Her. A traitor and a liar was the fiend!
His lechery is proved beyond dispute.
Two witnesses have testified his guilt,
The Greek of Sparta being one of them.
This man no grudge against the queen can have,
Supposing that our sister liked her not.
Oh, dear Pheroras, why desert me thus,
And love a man who was a slave to me!
  Pher. His blood is on his head; thy hands are pure.
  Her. And she shall follow him who shared her bed;
No pity shall unfix my vengeful mind!　　[*Enter Phabatus.*
Who would see me? Who wishes to be seen?
Admit no man; I rather met an ape.
  Phab. My lord, the High Priest, Matthias, praying waits
That he with thy consent may see the queen.—
  Her. The strumpet—what with her? Still sympathy
With her, though outcast, not with me, the king!
The herb that makes beloved where is it found?
Like Hermon's dew man's love is Heaven's gift,
For crowns and sceptres can the heart not force.—
Mariamne, oh Mariamne, fallen, fallen,
An angel fallen from a glorious height;
If there be seraphim they weep thy fall.—
My queen!—A harlot she—my wife a wretch,
Condemned, imprisoned—perdition on
My head if I forgive her crime!—Go tell
The priest that mercy's gates are closed, and hell
Is yearning to devour the lusty drab!　　[*Exit Phabatus.*
  Pher. Oh brother, king, thy health, thy rest, thy peace
Are gone; thou art not more the same, the man
Of stern resolves, indomitable will
Can such a woman such a hero break!
She has no love for thee nor feeling for
Thy dearest friends. This land is rich in maids

Of rarest qualities and grace. Nor lives
A sovereign on this planet's round who would
Not willingly his daughter make thy wife.
   Her. Ah, lad! thy maids!—Speak not of maids; the sun's
Eternal radiance beams not on a face,
A figure and an eye like hers. Leave me,
Pheroras, I must be alone—in gloom,
In darkness, drear, despondency alone.
Mariamne's doom no power can revoke.
She dies—leave me alone.—Mariamne dies.   [*Exit Pheroras.*
Send Diophantus here—Mariamne dies.—
She falls, though with her Herod's fortune sinks!—
Last night I had a dream in which I saw
Her in supernal glory wrapt, the priests,
Her brother and Hyrcanus, by her side,
All radiating with effulgence pure.
I from a distance deep and drear did eye
Their lofty flight athwart the empyrean
Ablaze with glowing stars. Discerning me
Afar, methought, they frowned, when under me
The ground did open vast and horrid, and,
Amid demoniac yells and grisly shapes,
Who struck their talons in my writhing flesh,
I sinking deep and deeper fell with sense
Of guilt which agonized my thrilling soul.—
It was a dreadful phantom fancy wove
Out of the fever raging in my brains.—
They say there is somewhere an Eden for
The virtuous soul, and for the reprobates
There is a judgment and a racking hell.
If there be tortures in eternity
They equal not the agonies I bear
Alive!—Fools, dupes!—torture what is mud and wind!
Of mire, wind and water made, we live
On what they yield combined until the flesh
Outworn dissolves, and here the story ends.—
Her loathing lowered me in my esteem
So that, while she degraded in the jail
Is locked, I in my visions see her in
The fields of bliss, so mighty dominates
Her magic in my heated nerves.—" Deny
It, monster, or my loathing bear!" Ay, drab,
Thy loathing's arrows Herod can sustain,
But not a second time thou Herod shalt disdain.—
Thou, Diophantus, shalt my order bear;   [*Enter Diophantus.*
The captain of the jail will do the rest.
   Dio. I humbly serve thy pleasure, king; command.
   Her. See that before the sun completes his course
The queen be headless and inhumed straightway.
   Dio My king——
   Her. [*sardonic*] My king—my dog—compassion, what?
   Dio. I am thy slave, but this tremendous act!—
   Her. Tremendous fool! I charge thee, if thy life
Hath value—do what I command!—Woe, woe
Mariamne—night, abysm, horrid, O, O! |*Exit Herod.*
   Dio. Deplorable king, he knows not what he doth,
And reason's light appears in him eclipsed.

Yet disobey I dare not his behest;
Of all he slew the queen is sure the best.
Unearthly vengeance hovers over him;
The skies revolt and Herod's end is dim!   [*Exit Diophantus.*

SCENE II.

MARIAMNE *and* MATTHIAS, *in jail.*

Matt. So died he innocent of every guilt
With thee, my princess, who art thus accused?
Mari. So may Almighty all my sins forgive
As he was guiltless of the odious crime
For which he bloody execution bore.
His was a loyal and devoted soul,
And I am grieved at his untimely death;
And thou, dear sir, his memory wilt clear
Of shameful imputations put on him.
Matt. And thine illustrious self untainted stands
By this assertion made before thy end.
Mari. Before the threshold of eternity
I stand prepared the verdict of that Judge
To hear, who reads the naissant secrets of
Man's inmost breast, and in this solemn hour
I pledge my soul's eternal bliss that naught
But truth I told thee, sir, in all regards.
Calumniated Joseph lost his life
And spotless name, and I depart this world
A victim of imbruted tyranny
Matt. Among the martyrs of our sainted sires
Thou wilt, dear daughter, ever live and shine.
All-seeing Heaven will thy wrongs avenge.
He, though long-suffering, the wicked smites
With all the terrors of His burning wrath!
Mari. May He the father's crime not visit on
My children, whose career opes darker than
My end! My babes! auspicious Power guard
My babes by cutting short their years, since naught
Save gloom and woes the future breeds for them!
Matt. Thy gloom expires and thy day begins,
And they who live the Lord will not forsake.—
Daughter, enlarge thy sentiments, thy mind's
Celestial qualities distend, and part
In peace with pardon for thy blinded foes;
For such a triumph over passion won
Endues the spirit with upsoaring speed
When rid of clay it scales the azure's deep
To join the Source of which it is a ray.
How long soever man may here sojourn,
He thither must return whence he does come,
For here to stay not sent is the earth-born
Who vainly seeks below a blissful home.
          [*Captain and guards appear in the background.*]
Mari. [*inspired*] A high priest's daughter am I and, resigned,
I banish wrath and vengeance from the mind.
Forgiving all my foes I will depart
Propitiation mild within my heart.
[*Ecstatically*] I see my sires in divine array

Amid the chorists of the starlit heights,
Their sacred radiance to my gaze display;
Their eyes outsparkle the cerulean lights.
They beckon me to leave the earth in haste,
To wing with them through empyrean space;
I come, I come to share your blissful race
Ah, of your blessedness I long to taste.
I hear the symphonies which move the skies
So sweet and soft that cherubim do weep,
The spheres resounding their dominion keep,
The saintly hosts respond the melodies.
Ah, let me flee this dark terrestial vale
Where sorrows teem and joys are half and rare,
Where budding blossoms rifling nips the gale,
And sweetest hopes end in untold despair!—
  Enter DIOPHANTUS *and maids who bring two babes.*
These are my babes, my earthly hopes were these,
The Lord his blessings may on them bestow;
With my departure may their sorrows cease,
Adieu, my friends, my soul is freed from woe.
Adieu, my babes, take this your mother's kiss; [*Kissing them.*
We meet, my babes, and weep in realms of bliss.
[*She kisses the children again and again, then proceeds to the
 door where the captain and guards are waiting all the time.
 She is accompanied by Matthias, Diophantus, and the maids,
 two of whom take out the children through another door.
 The movements are solemn and mournful. A muffled drum
 is heard behind the scene.*]

SCENE III.

*The main portal of the Temple on which the Roman eagle is seen.
 A crowd of scholars with hatchets hidden under their cloaks.*

Enter JUDAS SARIPHEUS. SABION *appears watching at a distance.*

 J. Sarip. Be patient, children, patient till he comes,
He cannot longer tarry who should lead;
He is your master, act not rashly, boys.
 1st Schol. We wait resolved to shatter that fell bird
Yon perched in defiance of our God.
It is idoltary we foster in
Our midst.—Perish Herod, death or victory!
 2d Schol. That is the Roman eagle he set up
To pave the way for idols to come next.
Antiochus he likens every way.
 3d Schol. Tush, lest the Temple's guard take note of us
And in the germ suppress our brave resolve.
A throng of worshippers the precincts crowd
Who should the deed perceive when it is done
Not premature betray us to the chief,
Who will come running with his warlike pack.
 J. Sarip. The guards are doubled by the king's command,
Who fears an uproar since the queen is locked.—
Now there he nears and, somewhat hasty, too. [*Enter Matthias.*
What are thy news?—How is the queen, alive?
 Matt. Mariamne fell, I saw her severed head.
An angel fell, our manhood is disgraced.

Who for a slavish life such shame endure.
The tyrant slew the queen and we are mute,
Obedient, cringing, weeping, craven, mean!
Such days I will not see a second time.
My sorrow hath no bound. Oh, virtuous queen,
Oh, worthy daughter of a glorious race
How art thou fallen noble, great, resigned
To Heaven's decree, forgiving all, all, all!
   J. Sarip. Not him, she could not, should not him forgive.
Matt. She could and should that murderer forgive,
Who lost his senses, having lost his hopes.
   J. Sarip. We are not good enough to hear the best.—
Matt. No, no; the best would be his death—he lives
And may yet all of us survive.—But you
Are armed, children, and I waste your time.
   J. Sarip. They want that eagle down if thou sayst, yes.
Matt. That eagle?—Boys are you prepared to die?
Scholars. We are!
   Matt.   The Holy One be blessed,—I die
With you.—Bring down the image from the gate. [*They prepare.*
Wait, sons; some from the upper window must
By ropes descend till they the idol reach.—   [*Many rush in.*
Assist us, Heaven, in our pious work!
We bore it long, but now our patience ends.
To fall for Thee is what Thy Law commands!
[*Scholars descend by ropes from an upper window, reach the eagle*
    and strike it down. A crowd rushes out of the Temple.]
   1st Schol. [*smites the fragments*] So evil thing, that perch is
    not for thee!
Ay, trample on it, let the tyrant burst
With rage!—To atoms smash it, so. so, so!
[*The scholars smash it with their hatchets, the crowd trample on*
   the fractures; noise and laughter.]
   A Voice. The guard, the guard! Flee friends, flee!
    [*The crowd disperse. Judas, Matthias and scholars remain.*
     Enter Captain and guard, Sabion draws nearer.
   Capt.   Oh, sacrilege
And treason! The ensign smashed, the instruments
The High Priest's pupils hold with clinching grasp!—
My duty bids me to lay hand on you
At once. You all must guarded be until
The king has judged this foul revolt. Even
The High Priest cannot be exempt.—Thou art
Not of these rebels, for I saw thee come,
While others took to flight; who was the head
Of this outrageous, daring act?   [*To Sabion.*
   Matt.   By me
Encouraged they this idol shattered, which
The king, despite of Israel's sacred Law,
To please the heathen robbers, there did plant.
Lead on, I follow thee and shall this speech
As plainly to the king repeat as I
Did here, and let him judge me as he likes.
   Sab. It was a hasty deed I do regret,
And may the king provoke to be severe.
   Matt. Thy outward, Sabion, mirrors not thy mind;
We know thee better than thou know'st thyself.

J. Sarip. By thine devices old Hyrcanus died.

Capt. Let Sabion go, but you must follow me. [*Exit Sabion.*
My orders are not lenient in this case.—
Convey these prisoners to the citadel
The while I hasten to inform the king.
[*The Captain leaves, while the guards surround the prisoners.*

SCENE IV.

A room at Herod's.

Enter HEROD.

Herod. He died unguilty of the crime, he said.—
His wife did lie and I was maddened by
Mean jealousy.—The queen was innocent—
Mean jealousy!—Am I not mad!—Ah, if
My queen unguilty die—unguilty she
And I her murderer!—Ye spinners of
The mortal's earthly fate, ye powers black
Or white, ye fearful Destinies—if she
Be innocent—her blood, Mariamne's blood
Flowing guiltless—beheaded my love!—No!
She lives yet, sure she lives!—A messenger!
My voice affrights me—slaves, a messenger!—
Give me a messenger of lightning's speed! [*Enter Sabion.*
The heavens are gracious—man, what leads thee here
When crown and kingdom for thy like I gave?
Sab. My lord, the High Priest and a crowd of scholars——
Her. Hold, life and death depend upon thy haste,
Thy turn of tongue—run, she must not die!—
Sab. My sovereign, who not die?
Her.   Devil, the queen,
My wife! Dull-minded rogue, my wife! Stand not,
Thy errand will the headsman's axe arrest!—
Sab. The graces be with her!—   [*Exit.*
Her. [*wildly*]   Ha, ha, ha, ha, ha, ha!
The Fates are sullen and my star is red!
If it be done then Mercury would speed
In vain!—Thou, what, about the queen?   [*Captain enters.*
Capt. A crime rebellious in its kind was just
Committed at the Sanctuary's front.
Her. The stars rebel, why should my subjects bear
The yoke of tyranny on them enforced!—
What is the deed rebellious in thine eyes?—
Capt. The eagle from the portal's top they tore,
Incited by Matthias to revolt,
Who deems the ensign an idolatrous,
Abominable image; seeking fame
In martyrdom he counts his punishment
Would certainly involve.
Her.   It is a scratch
Disdainful to resent, while over me
Suspended is the hand of vengeful fates.—
That messenger's report I dread—she lives?   [*Enter Sabion.*
Sab. [*with downcast look*] My lord—
Her.   She lives? Say, yes!
Sab. [*as before*] My king—
Her. [*drawing nearer, the hand on his dagger*]   She lives?

Sab. The revocation came too late.—
Her. [*stabbing Sabion*] Liar,
She lives!—Open hell this murderer to receive!
   Sab. [*while Herod rushes out*] Oh, vilest monster thou—I feel
   my death
Is near; he struck my heart.—Hyrcanus now
Thy frowning ghost is by this gore appeased!—
Vile tyrant—help me, Heaven—friend—my wife—
My children—tell them—oh, I sink.—   [*He dies.*
   Capt.   The king
Is mad and things rush to a turn. I hear
Some voices.—Sabion slain, of late abhorred
By many and by others feared.—Through him,
They said, Hyrcanus was betrayed, and he
Betrayed his treason ere he died.—Who comes?
       Enter PHERORAS, EURYCLES, PHABATUS *and* SALOME.
   Pher. The king away and Sabion in his blood,
What happened here thou wast a witness of?
   Capt. I stand in terror, prince, of what I saw.
This man fell stabbed by our dreadful king,
On bringing tidings of our queen's demise.
   Pher. And whither went the king this being done?
   Capt. In that direction rushed he in despair.
   Pher. [*to Phabatus*] Be near the king, I tremble for his life.
                    [*Exit Phabatus.*
And, captain, thou thy quarter keep in peace
And re-enforce thy guards, for now the night
Descends and all is restless in the town.
Remove this body in the twilight's dusk.—
He died not innocent, this guileful rogue.
      [*The captain and Eurycles remove the body.*
   Sal. She is yet ruling from her grave the king.
If he persist how may this mania end?
   Pher. His blood is at its boiling heat, it must
Cool down or he demented sink; meanwhile
The cares of state my rest disturb. From end
To end the country is in flames, revolt
And disaffection stirring every tribe;
And hydra-headed is the plotters' crowd.—
A strong patrol this city guards to-night,
While to the palace none can entrance have,
Save friends disarmed and our servants known.
No caution seems superfluous in such state
Of things.—And thou, Salome, be the king's
Propitious nurse. Forsake not, sister, him
In overpowering grief.—I cannot stay.
   Sal. His fits of madness make me dread his sight;
When these survene he knows not what he doth,
                  [*Phabatus re-enters.*
And life is scarce secure within his reach.
   Pher. How does the monarch?
   Phab.   Weeps, dear prince; outstretched
Upon the queen's pavilioned bed he groans
And unintelligibly talking vents
His pains.—" Mariamne, answer—guiltless—love
And murder—" are his uttered words.—I durst
Not budge, but quietly withdrew.

Pher. The tears
Of poignant sorrows will his heart relieve.
What soothing remedy could we apply
To quell the fury of his feverish blood?
A wise physician could his nerves subdue
By some ingredients known to magic art.
   Phab. I know a man who nature's secrets steals,
And by his subtlety incurable
Distempers cured. A word will bring him straight.
   Pher. Go in my name request the skilful man
To use his art in quieting the king.—   [*Phabatus leaves.*
Thou with the Greek be present when he comes
An₁ go not hence until I take thy place.—
I charge the guards thy orders to obey.   [*Exit Pheroras.*
   Sal. Believe or not believe a monitor
There is in us, whose warning voice the soul
Affrights not less than fulminating claps
Descending fire-laden from the skies!—
The shrew is dead, why shudder at her name
Who from the bowels of earth can never rise
To prove the guile of my successful scheme?
And where I am, awake, asleep, by day,
By night, I see my husband's bloodless face
Distorted, ghastly, pitiful, terrific!
Of Pluto's hellish brood the blackest in
Her fiendish ways is Vengeance, restless, dark,
Destructive, bloody, horrid, hateful, foul!—
The Greek did with his lies disgust me, though
By me instructed he did meanly lie,
And my achievement is to be the whore
Of such a scurvy liar as he is.—
Oh Vice, I see thy varnish'd ugliness,
But all the pathways to remorse are blocked.
What crime is crime remains; the dead are dead
Who through me died, but guilt weighs down my head.
There is no pardon for a wretch like me,
No brand too gross for my ignominy.   [*Exit.*

SCENE V.

Herod's Bedchamber.

He is seen in a trance on his bed; around him stand a physician
PHABATUS, DIOPHANTUS, SALOME *and* EURYCLES.

   Physician. [*holding a case full of pills and vials in hand*]
     This casus puzzles my prodigious brains,
Imbued with wisdom of the sacred pages
Of what Asclepius taught and Egypt's sages
In sounding man's diseases and his pains,
How they spring up, evolve and force the breath
Out of the mortal's frame, which fools call death;
For in great nature's workings nothing dies,
And earth is ever young, as are the skies.—
With Hippocratic skill I thousands cured
Phlegmatic humors withered for the grave,
And if three-fourth untimely death endured,
It was by accident through drugs I gave;

The physicus his art must boldly try
On morbid systems, though the patients die.—
This case encloses herbs from every clime,
Of magic power nature to revive,
They, joined to the cure of healing time,
Can all the morbi from the body drive;
But here is one which, since from Eden driven
Mankind is sinning, is but found in heaven.—
Let me apply it to the sufferer's head
Whose vital current now a fever heats,
Whose pulse, I feel, a fearful tempo beats,
And even if he lifeless were as dead
This medicine will in his mind create
A wondrous stir which will, at any rate,
Mysterious visions bring before his sight
And soothe his sorrows with the parting night.
                    [*He applies the herb to Herod's head.*
And now, dear princess, let no breathing thing
Disturb the rest of the despondent king.
In the adjoining room you quiet keep,
While he reposing tastes the balm of sleep.

[*Exeunt all. The lights are lowered; a strain of soft music is
    heard; on a brilliant chariot Hyrcanus. Mariamne, and
    Aristobulus with harps in hand and dazzling wings glide by
    in the air, their smiles vanish at seeing Herod.   They
    disappear; the music ceases, whereupon thunder and light-
    ning burst from the ground, followed by a black crew of
    tailed and horned goblins yelling, laughing, and gnashing
    their teeth at Herod's sight, and vanishing in the dark.*]

   Her. [*upstarting*] I sink—I fall—am lost—gracious powers,
My soul—the goblins—dread and blackness!—Ha,
Mariamne an angel—they I slew with her
And I forever wretched, damned, lost!—
No, phantom—I was dreaming; no, she lives!
My queen lives!—This is her bed—my bed—oh
Felicity, Mariamne's bed!—Come love,
My angel—Ha!—Mariamne! Mariamne!—Slaves,
My queen, where is my queen?—Mariamne, ho!
Deserters, all asleep—I want my queen!   [*Eurycles enters.*
Where is my wife, my beauteous queen? I want
Her, call her!—Why hesitate?—Obedience, thug!
Give ear for Herod speaks—am I the king?
   Eury. My lord!——
   Her.   Thou wouldst not stir—where is my queen?
   Eury. Thou knowest where, my king.—She will not come.
   Her. Not come if I command, beseech, implore!
Not come if I forgive and love and kiss,
And kneel and worship her, not come!—   [*Enter Salome.*
   Eury.   My lord,
Her ears are deaf, she will not hear my voice.
   Sal. Oh Lord——
            [*Pherorus, Diophantus, Phabatus, and Corinthus Enter.*
   Her.   Not come!—let me talk to him—deaf
She is, he said, and will not come,—she must,
She will—she is not dead, my wife?—
   Eury.   She is!—

Her. [*stabs Eurycles*] This for thy evil-forging tongue—she
    lives!—   [*All are startled.*
Move not or he who moves will move the last!
  Eury. The furies tear thy soul, ferocious brute!   [*He sinks.*
I breathe the last; the freezing chills of death
Rush through my veins, my sight grows dim—but hear
And swallow poison worse than vipers spit.—
Thy queen, fierce monster, died without a stain!
  Her. Ha, daggers are thy words yet speak, I hear!
  Sal. Infamous liar what wilt thou forge to sting
A credulous man?
  Eury.   Infamous wretch, thou shalt
This time the truth hear!—By the dreadful gods
Who on my head Mariamne's innocence
And fair Aristobulus' blood avenge,
Herod, I shall the truth divulge, or may
From Pluto's blackest regions never rise
My soul!
  Her.   Divulge and let the furies tear
Me now that I my seraph murderously
Slew. Angelic image—innocent my love—
Defamed and struck and guiltless—O, O, O!
My babies of their heavenly nurse bereaved,
My sweetest, godliest, gentlest beauteous queen
Beheaded—fallen, fallen—O, my heart!—
    [*He lays his hands on his breast in a state of extreme agony.*
  Eury. She died an honest woman loyal to
Thy bed, and he, that strumpet's husband, he
The best was of thy choicest friends; he did
Not what, to please thy sister, I did say.—
She Joseph forced thy secret to divulge,
And with her virtue paid my slanderous task.—
  Sal. Demoniac liar!   [*She wants to run away.*
  Her.   Hold, infernal, or this
My weapon will transpierce thy hateful breast!   [*To Salome.*
Woe, woe!—My dream, my fear, my queen, my love!   [*Weeps.*
  Eury. My time is out.—Thy wife was innocent,
Her foe thy sister; I her instrument,
Who shared Salome's bed while Joseph lived.
    [*Eurycles dies; Salome hides her face; Pheroras turns away.*
  Her. Chaos and darkness;—Men, why stand ye still?
When yonder wretch I slew you stirred all
But this enormous guilt and my sweet wife's,
Your queen's destruction kindles not your blood,
Arouses not your manhood to a pitch
Of vengeance on a fiendish, horrid ghoul!
Ah, all the sorrows and the shame is mine,
The Lord of heavens is a fearful Judge!—
Mariamne, cherub, yea, thou art no more,
The earth did swallow thy celestial frame;
Through me they shed thy guiltless, sweetest gore,
Thou art in Heaven, mine is dole and shame.
But longer whelming woes I can't sustain,
They must in madness, self-destruction end,
For never bore one breast such loads of pain
As from above upon my head descend.
The stars, the Fates are waging war with me,

A broken mortal how shall I contend
With them who strike and wound invisibly
When with their deathful shafts they bosoms rend.—
But if they think that Herod hath no nerves
To breast the onslaught of malicious fates,
They shall now find that Herod never swerves
From grimly death and black Abaddon's gates!—
Behold, my friends, I slew so dear a wife
That Heaven's treasures could not pay her worth;
I thirst for vengeance not, but hate this life
And gracious Heaven gave us—this on earth!

[*He tries to stab himself, Pheroras falls in his arms.   While the
    curtain descends a voice is heard; "He lives, a prey to guilt-
    ful shame!"*